INTERFAITH MARRIAGE
Pastoral Concerns

INTERFAITH MARRIAGE
Pastoral Concerns

Lengmi Lungleng

2019

INTERFAITH MARRIAGE: Pastoral Concerns – Published by the Rev. Dr. Ashish Amos of the Indian Society for Promoting Christian Knowledge (ISPCK), Post Box 1585, Kashmere Gate, Delhi-110006.

Online Order: http://ispck.org.in/book.php

ISBN: 978-93-88945-01-1

Laser typeset by

ISPCK, Post Box 1585, 1654, Madarsa Road, Kashmere Gate, Delhi-110006 • *Tel:* 23866323

e-mail: ashish@ispck.org.in • ella@ispck.org.in
website: www.ispck.org.in

Dedicated to
my late brother Shangreisui Lungleng
who encouraged, inspired and motivated me.

Contents

Acknowledgement

I would like to acknowledge the support and inspirational spirit of my mentors, colleagues and family members, through whom I could sustain my theological journey. Also, I am grateful to the Senate of Serampore College (University) for permitting me to publish my thesis into book.

Foreword

The issue of marital satisfaction and moral codes in marriage is always a topic of interest among researchers. The perplexity of Christian morality is unquestionably in the limelight as we discuss the issue of mixed marriages. Indian society is still traditional and religious in comparison to any western societies. Most of the Indian marriages are arrange marriage where the parents have a great say in the decision making of family life to the young generation. Marrying someone from a different cultural or religious background could invite a lot of fuss and fume in the family and society. Churches take disciplinary measures upon those who are married to someone from a different religion. It is in this context that the issue of mixed marriages creates a challenge to ministers and counsellors. Lengmi Lungleng deserves a special appreciation as he has done a detailed study on the psycho social problems of couples who got married from different religious backgrounds.

There are various issues of concern regarding mixed marriages. Different churches have different views in handling this issue. The basic fact of concern is the perplexity of their identity. It is expected of mixed marriages to blend smoothly despite the distinct cultural, moral, ethical and epistemological differences due to the difference in faith and religious practices. There are always chances of disparity in world view, disparity in value system among people who marry from different religious and cultural backgrounds. The very outlook to the social custom and practices too may differ here.

In many cases, mixed marriage may lack societal and familial support and then the couple from interfaith marriage will have to struggle with the emotional turbulence due to the cutting of the codes of love from family and relatives. The role of the church comes when the couples seek help from the congregation they are affiliated with. There comes the role of the church. The churches have been keeping a very negative attitude to those couples of mixed marriages. Churches do not accept them in to the love and fellowship of the members and many keep a negative attitude to them. This may create an indifferent or sometimes rebellious attitude to God and spirituality among couples of interfaith marriages. A Christian minister or a skilled helper may have to deal with this spiritual reality as they minister to couples of this background.

In order to escape from the societal and religious seclusion, some couples of interfaith marriages tend to amplify the inter personal bond of love so tightly that they feel so close to each other due to these challenges. But the situation is grave when there is less emotional control and less level of tolerance maintained in the family. They are challenged by the tension creating situations in and around their surroundings and they are expected to overcome those special situations and also the attitude of the "malignant" society around. Some adjust well and cannot and the family breaks apart.

It is also a reality when the children of interfaith marriages struggle with their cultural and religious identity. The situation is worse when one of the parents decide a different religious value system and identity and want to impose the same upon the child/

children without consultation. This can possibly create confusion to children and then it can be transferred to the parents as well. This creates another area of struggle and stress among couples of interfaith marriages.

I am so happy that Lengmi Lungleng has come up with some solid understanding based upon the empirical datas. These insights drawn from the practical exposure to the lives of couples from interfaith marriage will be a great source for Christian ministers and counsellors. Family counselling is one of the areas which we require many writings in India. Some of the social realities like this in Indian societies must find a relevant space in writings. Only then we will be able to come up with an approach of counselling which is relevant for the unique Indian society.

Dr. Saji Kumar K.P. Principal
India Baptist Theological Seminary
Kottayam, Kerala

Preface

As the world is developing day by day, it brings lots of changes in all dimension, particularly in the value and significance of Christian marriage life. As this becomes one of the reasons, people are confused of the Christian morality, particularly of Christian marriage. To be clear of Christian marriage, one should always base on Biblical teaching. In Pluralistic societies which is characterized by different religious and ethnic backgrounds, it becomes common for people to fall in love, enter into marriage and establish families. When there is interfaith marriage, the sanctity of Christian marriage is lost and there is less possibility to perform Christian wedding amid God's people and in the name of God. After all, majority of the families or couples of interfaith marriages are going through many difficulties to uphold a successful married life because of the differences in culture, traditions, life styles and religions. As a result, they face several Psychological and social problems. Amid such crisis, it is a Christian steward's responsibility to reach through Pastoral care and Counselling.

Lengmi Lungleng
Assistant Professor,
Yavatmal College for Leadership Training
Yavatmal, Maharashtra

CHAPTER - 1

Introductory Understanding of Interfaith Marriage

There is a rapid growth rate of interfaith marriages all over the world. Many young people knowingly and sometimes willingly leave their own religious identity and opt for interfaith marriages. This is one of the evidences of declining role of faith and religious identity in the minds of many young people. Sometimes, they do not wish to identify themselves with any religion but they rather hold on their identity by their profession as a mere human being . The world has become smaller as people travel easily across regions for various reasons and meet different local people. Many end up marrying them regardless of religious affiliation. These are the fact that the present world is facing. The deeper understanding will be revealed by exploring 'marriage', types of marriage, biblical views on interfaith marriages, causes and effects related to the couples of interfaith marriages.

Marriage

Etymology of the term 'marriage'

The term 'marriage' stems from the ancient Latin word, *Maritus*, which means husband. The word 'matrimony' also has Latin origin, *matrimonium,* meaning 'mother'. Family is the most important and precious institution of which God is the author and founder. It is the normal place where young people grow to moral and spiritual maturity. It is the cradle of life and love, the place in which a person is born and brought up.[1] The common Hebrew term *laqah* "to take in marriage," should be seen in association with the verb *ba'al,* "to be master, rule, or possess in marriage," as well as with the noun *ba'al,* "master, lord, husband." A comparable Greek verb would be *gameo,* "to marry, take to wife," along with its cognate forms *gamizo* and *gamisko,* both meaning "to give in marriage." The Old Testament views marriage as a natural state for the adult human. Marriage is so expected that the Hebrew word that indicates "husband" is simply *ish,* which means "a man." And the word translated both "wife" and "marriage" is *'isah.* One aspect of being an adult male is to be a husband, and one aspect of being an adult female is to be a wife.[2]

Definitions of Marriage

Marriage may be defined as lifelong and exclusive state in which a man and woman are wholly committed to live with the other in sexual relationship under conditions normally approved and witnessed to by their social group or society.[3] The essence of marriage is two persons seeking to form a more perfect life through giving themselves totally to each other. Santhosh John quoted the definition of Friedrich Nietzsche that defined marriage as "the will of two to create the one who is greater than they who create." "Therefore, a man leaves his father and his mother and clings to his wife, and they become one flesh" (Gen. 2:24), so they are no longer two but one flesh (Matt. 19:6). Two have become one, an expression of the heart of marital love. Marriage is more than an agreement between a man and a woman to live together, more than a mutual exchange of promises of support and comfort, more than an agreement to observe the civil and ecclesiastical laws of marriage, more than a promise to help each other achieve union with God.[4]

Marriage is one of the universal social institutions. It is a socially approved way of establishing a family of procreation. It is a relatively permanent bond between permissible mates.[5] "Marriage is a vital social institution." Like all social institutions, marriage is constituted by a unique web of shared public meanings. For important institutions, including marriage, many of those meanings rise to the level of norms. Such social institutions affect individuals profoundly; institutional meanings and norms teach, form, and transform individuals, supplying identities, purposes, practices, and projects.[6] Marriage is a divinely ordained union with a moral purpose. When a man and a woman decide to unite in marriage God gives them responsibilities related to married life.[7] Because, God himself planned the idea of marriage, therefore, marriage is of God, a divine institution.

When two persons are united by marriage in God, they then form but a single creature in the eyes of God, and God himself enters that union with them. It is not simply a contract of mutual fidelity; the Lord himself achieves that mysterious union of husband and wife. The work of God, who unites husband and wife in him, is his response to a human undertaking initially founded on the love of man and woman. Marriage is constituted by the union of two persons, in God by God, made public by a ceremony in the Church and attested by the words of Christ, they are no more two, but one flesh. What God has joined together, let no one separate" (Matt. 19:4-5).[8] It means cohabitation that involves the life, the work and the interest of the partners. It is based on a community of life that embraces and gives security to the persons and becomes enlarged into a community for the begetting and raising of children.[9] In a true marriage, the unity of husband and wife will reflect the eternal unity of Christ and his Church. It is not only a bond between one man and one woman, because it is sealed by the greater bond of unity with God and his people. This bond must always come first.[10]

Types of marriages

Arranged marriage

This type of marriage is arranged and settled by the parents with the co-operation of the relatives and friends. The match selection may be through the attribution of caste, abilities, character, education, social status, age etc. the traditional values of an arranged match are within the caste itself.[11]

Love marriage

In this marriage a man and a woman choose their partner for marriage. It may be with or without the approval of the parents. It is normally noticed that love marriage is good because it helps the partners to know each other before they marry. But some say that, it is not successful because it is not based on a mature decision.[12]

Arranged love marriage

In this type of marriage, parents, other elders and man and woman play a major role in approval and disapproval of marriage. In this arranged love marriage, youngsters choose their partners according to their likes and marry with the approval of the parents. In this marriage youths get the freedom to select their partners and receive blessings from their parents and loved ones.[13]

Inter caste marriage

In this marriage both the girl and boy come from different castes. Every caste gives importance to their caste structures and want all people to marry within the structures of the caste. The Law gives all rights for inter-caste marriage, but parents and relatives may not give their approval for inter caste marriage. The prejudice of the society is the root cause against this type of marriage.[14] Dr Lizy James, a social scientist says, "Inter-caste marriage can be understood as including both marriages between major castes, such as a marriage between a Brahmin and Kshatriya, and marriages between sub-castes within a major caste group, such as a marriage between people of different Brahmin sub-castes".[15]

Interfaith marriage

Marriage between people of two faiths or two different religions is called inter faith marriage. The term Interfaith-marriage literally used to identify couples who do not practice the same religion. This term typically refers to separate faiths. Marriages that consist of a Christian and a Muslim or a Hindu and an atheist would be considered as interfaith marriage. Interfaith marriage is a phenomenon built on the choice of two individuals to share a life while acknowledging the difference between them in terms of their religious backgrounds, beliefs, and practices.[16]

Marriages between Hindus and Muslims faces the most opposition. Professor of Sociology and Chair of the Centre for the Study of Social Systems at the Jawaharlal Nehru University, in correspondence with the Research Directorate, stated that marriages between a Hindu boy and a Muslim girl are particularly problematic compared to other inter-religious couples. The sociologist further noted that Hindus from higher castes were likely to experience more opposition to an inter-religious marriage than Hindus from lower castes. In addition, the sociologist stated that marriages between Hindus and Christians were less problematic (indeed they too faced problems), and Christians (a boy) who inter-marry from other religion, although they may face disapproval, they were unlikely to face violence from their families. The interfaith marriage couple settled in urban areas experienced less discrimination than those settled in rural areas. She said that inter-religious couples from rural areas who experience problems with their families or villagers often move to urban areas where there is more tolerance. In urban areas it would be more difficult to identify inter-faith couples. Even where an inter-faith couple is identified, it is not likely they would face serious hardship.[17]

The *Special Marriage Act 1954* provides for civil marriage, including civil marriage between people of different religions. The National Portal of India website, the official website that acts as an access point for information about Indian government services, explains that the *Special Marriage Act* applies to all of India except Jammu and Kashmir State. The *Special Marriage Act* does not require a marriage to include any religious rituals or ceremonies and does not require either party to convert to the others religion. In May 2011, the Department of Foreign Affairs and Trade (DFAT) advised that: India is officially a secular and multi-ethnic country. Inter-religious marriage is legal in India. The *Special Marriage Act* of 1954 is an optional law in India and an alternative to each of the various religious personal laws. The *Special Marriage Act* is available to all citizens who choose to marry outside their faith. Religion of the parties to an intended marriage is immaterial under the Act. The *Special Marriage Act* does require that the parties are not blood or adopted relatives (unless there is a cultural custom governing at least one of the parties which permits of a marriage between them), and that the male be a minimum of twenty-one years of age and the female a minimum of eighteen years of age.[18]

Marriage in biblical history

Biblical concepts of marriage cannot divorce its history. In biblical times commonly, polygamous, monogamous, endogamous and levirate systems were practiced.

Polygamous system of marriage

The word polygamous is a system of marriage where a husband has more than one wife. From the time of Lemech the son of Cain until King Hammurabi, polygamous system of marriage was common, particularly among the aristocrats. Kings in those days were boastful in having many wives and concubines which ultimately had troubles in their domestic affairs. Though polygamous marriage was practiced by self motivated persons it was only permitted as temporary measure. It is a denial of the principle of marriage between husband and wife being one flesh (noted in Genesis 2:24; Matthew 19:5); which led to immeasurable marital problems. Example can be stated with the case of Abraham and Jacob who had much sorrows because of this polygamous marriage. David and Solomon who married several wives ended their families' life in sorrowful and tragic manner (II Sam. 5:13, 14; I kings 11:1).[19]

Monogamous system of marriage

Monogamous system of marriage is one man for one woman, one woman for one man. The creation narrative (Gen. 2:24) makes this point with its call to the man to forsake his mother and father and cleave unto his wife (not wives). It is implicit in the story of Adam and Eve, since God created only one wife for Adam. Several laws have been cited as support for monogamous marriage.[20] God preserves the number of males practically equal to the number of females in nations.[21]

Endogamous system of marriage

Endogamous is the custom of marrying only within one's own group, such as clan, tribe and faith. This system of marriage is the norm in the patriarchal age.[22] This system illustrates the common phenomenon of cross-cousin marriage, i.e. Marriage between the offspring of siblings of opposite sex, one in which a man marries the daughters of his mother's brother, despite the close degree of constant correlation. The justifications for endogamy are clear enough. It could be based on such a thing as unfriendly relations with a neighboring tribe or it may signal a need for separation from a majority group while living among or adjacent to foreigners. It reflects the practical needs to preserve a certain norm of religious behavior and to maintain the ethnic purity of the tribe or family.[23]

Exogamous system of marriage

Exogamous is the custom of marrying outside one's own clan, tribe, nations and faith. There are many narratives where Jew men married women from other tribes, nations and faith.[24] Also there are narratives where Jew women married men from other tribes, nations and faith.[25] This system of marriage took place out of spite (Esau's), when one was living in a foreign land for an unusually long period of time (Joseph's, Moses', Esther's), with divine approval (but parent disapproval) as a means of moving against the enemy (Judges 13:3,4), for consolidation of political power (David's) and in blatant disregard for religious norms (Ahab's and Solomon's).[26]

Levirate system of marriage

The name is derived from Latin word *Levir*, meaning 'husbands' brother'. When a married man died without a child his brother was expected to take his wife, children of the marriage counted as the children of the first husband. The custom is found in the life of Onan (Gen. 38:8-10). Deut. 25:5-10 states the law as applying to brethren who dwell together but allows the brother the option of refusing. In the light of Levirate law, a man cannot marry his own brother's wife to be his own wife whether she has been divorced during her husband's lifetime or has been left with or without children at her husband's death. John the Baptist rebuked Herod Antipas for marrying the wife of his own brother Herod Phillip because Phillip was still alive (Matt. 14:3-4). The purpose of Levirate system of marriage is to insist on the duty of the survivor, to perform the duty of a husband's brother, it is to preserve the family's name, clan and inheritance and to prevent problems in division of properties.[27]

Parent arranged marriage

The Hebrews practice the parent arranged marriages. However, there is no law in the Deuteronomic code (Deut. 12-26) to the effect that it is the responsibility of a father to select a bride for his son. In the Old Testament wisdom literature, while having much to say about healthy marital relationships, never classifies as wise to one who chose a wife for his son with prudence. Indeed Proverbs 19:14 affirms that a good wife is from the Lord and not from the husband's father. The narratives of parent arranged marriage for their sons are found in the following.[28] Such arrangement focuses attention upon the entire family unit and not just on the couple alone. It permits an understanding of love which has much to do with the commitment of the will as it does with emotions, glands and hormones.[29]

Significance of marriage

Marriage is a part of God's creative plan for humankind. It is not merely a cultural habit which has developed in various ways according to people's needs in each society. Marriage means being united and living together to grow in unity of mind, spirit and body. This partnership in unity is the foundation of marital relationship. Marriage is not the result of a relationship but is the beginning by understanding God's divine purpose. Marriage is a gift of God. It is a unique and distinct covenant relationship through his glory and goodness.[30] It is a permanent bond between one man and one woman for bearing and rearing children. Generally, the purpose of marriage is three-fold: Companionship, procreation and parenthood.[31] Thus, significance of marriage aims at strengthening the very fabric of the family and thereby of the society and that religion is a support base for the institution of marriage. Considering the rights and dignity of both man and woman and the fundamental rights of the children to have the love and affection of the parents, unity and indissolubility are the two essential properties of marriage.[32]

Marriage is an institution established by God

Marriage is divinely ordained union with a moral purpose. When a man and a woman decide to unite in marriage God gives them responsibilities for a married life. It is the handiwork of God for the procreation, pleasure and preservation of human race.[33] After Adam was created, God says that it is not good for Adam to be alone, so he created Eve to be united with Adam (Gen. 2:18). Thus, the first marriage was instituted and established by God with his knowledge and blessing. Also, God's image becomes perfect when a man and a woman become one through the relationship of marriage.[34] Marriage was God's plan and not by humans. In a true sense, marriage is the participation in a union established by the creator himself. Marriage therefore, is a divine institution.

Marriage as union of two creatures

In marriage, a man and a woman are so closely joined that they become one flesh. Marriage is the welding of two people together into one unit, the blending of two minds, two wills, two sets of emotions and two spirits. They are not two anymore from the divine inception rather they became one (which is an invisible). The Lord intends the bond to be indissoluble if both partners are alive. Here the goal is the perfect oneness, both in the intimacy of the physical and in the intimacy of the spiritual.[35] In Genesis 2:23, man says that woman is "bone of my bones and flesh of my flesh…" it is a mere biological statement describing a blood relationship. It is an assertion about the original unity of man and woman as whole persons. It is a union of two individuals in both physical and psychological dimension. Therefore, married couples are no longer two but one flesh (Mt. 19:6). Whenever a couple unites in the act of intercourse it brings union of oneness. It is an expression of new reality created by God.[36]

Marriage as covenant relationship

Marriage is called a covenant throughout the Pentateuch and the rest of the Old Testament. A marriage covenant is also referred to in many of the passages that speak about a covenant with God. The word covenant may mean a marriage covenant or a treaty covenant. The primary meaning of covenant was an agreement between two parties that was mutually binding and of mutual concern and loyalty which was expressed as love, even in the treaty as well as marriage covenant. For Christians, a marriage contract is a covenant between three parties: the man, the woman and God.[37] Covenant implies a sacred pact involving personal and mutual commitment. Through the marital covenant, the spouse commits themselves to sharing their entire life together as a couple. Marriage is a covenant by which a man and woman establish between themselves a partnership of the whole life. The covenant of marriage is a commitment to the mutual responsibility for fulfilling the deep personality needs of the other to love and to cherish. Marriage is a mutual covenant, which is a God given obligation between a man and a woman to have lifelong companionship.[38] Marriage as a covenant is the ultimate bonding of lovers; it is the covenant between a husband and wife who commit themselves to each other in an arrangement, promising faithfully to respond to each other's needs and gift. It is a conditional covenant insured by God, where the husband promises to provide for the essential needs of the wife while the wife promises to be faithful to her husband. The joining is meant to be permanent and to involve commitment.[39]

Marriage as lifelong union

It is the most cherished institution of God and it is a beautiful relationship that God has established for a man and a woman to enjoy their lifetime together till death takes them apart. In marriage there is divine joining together, which requires obedience to God and his/her will that the union remain lifelong. It is also a mutual commitment of the partners. In marriage, couples must prepare to live with one another in a lasting community of life. It is a relationship of lifelong with mutual faithfulness. It is meant to be a permanent union and not a mere collection of rights and duties binding a man and woman as husband and wife. It is an interpersonal union between a man and a woman who have made commitments to each other, to live together which are recognized by society as lifetime bonds. It is constituted by the union of the two people, in God and by God, made public by a ceremony in the Church and attested by the words of Christ. So, they are no longer two but one, and their union is not for timing but for lifetime or for everlasting.[40]

Marriage as sacrament

Marriage is sacramental because it symbolizes the relationship between Christ and the Church. Paul in his letter to the Ephesians describes the relationship between husband and wife to the mystery of the relationship between Christ and the Church (Eph. 5: 25-33). The bond of love between husband and wife is not just dependent on physical attraction or other worldly considerations and natural family obligations. It has a spiritual dimension and for Christians the model for love is the love of God revealed in the sacrificial love of Christ which led him to the Cross. In marriage couples mutually commit themselves and surrender their marriage to symbolize the love of Christ. They also commit themselves to make the love of Christ the pattern for the love they practice in their lives.[41] By sacrament it means that marriage has become an outward sign of grace, instituted by Christ and conferring grace upon the recipient. Thus, the union of husband and wife in marriage is something wondrous and unique. It is an inspiring challenge to make their lives an extension of that intimate and loving union which exists between Christ and his Church.[42]

Marriage as mutual sacrifice

Marriage is a mutual sacrifice and self-giving love. The couple's relationship with Jesus is reflected and actualized in their most intimate and profound relationship with one another. They are under the authority of one another, for in their own self-renunciation to the Lord, they both find their true centre not in their own self but in the other. Jesus Christ sacrifices his life for the Church to show his deep and genuine love. Even in the life of husband and wife, there should be a spirit of sacrifice for his/her partner. Here the sacrifice is not only of physical but of desire, interest, belonging and spirituality. In marriage where there is emotional, physical and spiritual compatibility, nothing can shake the foundations of marriage. It is important to be sensitive to each other and share fears and anxieties or even resentment. Mutual respect and mutual surrender are essential.[43]

Interfaith-marriage in the Bible

The Bible talks about interfaith marriage. But one cannot categorically say that Bible gives only one perspective. The attempt here is not to take an extensive analytical or critical study of the passages or instances that talks about interfaith marriages, rather it is to make a survey of passages that indicate interfaith marriages. The effort is not to pick up a few biblical passages out of context and prove that the Bible speaks about interfaith marriages in one way or the other but rather to see the passages in their contexts and to see what they tell us.

Old Testament

Positive aspects

There are sets of passages which encourage or accept interfaith marriages. We know that Laban's household worshipped other gods. We also know that his daughter Rachel who became Jacob's wife followed the ways of her childhood religious lifestyles. In Genesis 31, we read that Rachel stole her father's household gods and put them under her saddle as she left her childhood home with Jacob. Jacob's twelve sons and one daughter, we see no concern from Jacob about intermarriage with local cultures. In Genesis 26:34 and 36:2, we are told that Esau married a Hittite woman. Both Judah (Gen. 38:1) and Simeon (Gen. 46:8) chose Canaanite wives and Joseph's wife, Asenath, was Egyptian (Gen. 41:45).[44]

While in Egypt Joseph married Asenath the daughter of the priest of On and through her he had two sons Manasseh and Ephraim (Gen. 41:50-52, 46:20). Both were accepted as heir to Joseph's family. Jacob, before his death, reckons with them and accepts them as his children: "Now then your two sons, born to you in Egypt before I came to you here will be reckoned as mine, Ephraim and Manasseh will be mine, just as Reuben and Simeon are mine" (Gen. 48:5-6), says Joseph.[45]

Judah, one of the sons of Joseph, married the daughter of a Canaanite by the name Shua. Judah also got his son Er to marry a Canaanite by name Tamar (Gen. 38:1-6). Moses had a Cushite wife (Num. 12:1) by named Zipporah, the daughter of a Midianite priest (Exo. 2:21). Miriam and Aaron spoke ill of Moses because he had a Cushite wife, but the subsequent passage holds Moses in high esteem. God takes Miriam and Aaron to task for speaking ill against Moses. Miriam was even punished for that. So, Moses marrying someone outside the fold was not seen as something unacceptable. Jeremiah too encouraged Israelites to marry into other faiths and have sons and daughters, find wives for the sons and gives daughters in marriage (Jer. 29:4-9). Thus, in the Old Testament there are some passages that give positive views on interfaith marriage.[46]

Negative aspects

On the other hand, there are also other sets of passages which discourage or go against interfaith marriages (Gen. 24:3; Ex.34:16; Ezra9:12; I Kings 11:2; Deut 7:3-4; Josh. 23:12-13). Such marriages were regarded as a source of unfaithfulness to the covenant and of sinfulness (I Kings 11:8-9; Deut. 7:3-4; Josh. 23:12-13; Mal. 2:10-11; Ezra 9:1-2; 10:2; 10:10; Neh. 10:28-30; 13:26-27). In the history of Israel after giving the second set of Ten Commandments, God asks Moses not to make any covenant with the local people and not to give their women to them to be their wives or to take their women to be wives of the Israelites. The reason suggested was that taking members from other religious faith might lead to worship of other gods (Exo. 34:12-16). It also says, "Do not inter-marry them (other nations). Do not give your daughters to their sons or take their daughters for your sons, for they will turn your sons away from following me to serve other gods…" (Deut. 7:3-4a).[47] The progeny of illegal marriages between Israelites and non-Israelites was described a bastard (Deut. 23:2).[48]

Ezra's plea against interfaith marriage is still stronger. The people confessed before Ezra that they had been unfaithful to their God by marrying foreign women from the people around them (Ezra 10:2). Therefore, Ezra made them confess to the Lord that they would do his will and separate themselves from the people around them (Ezra 10:11). Nehemiah also encouraged the Israelites to take an oath in God's name, "you are not to give your daughters in marriage to their sons, nor are you to take their daughters in marriage to your sons or for yourself" (Neh. 13.25). His fear was that the foreign wives could lead them into sin (Neh. 13:26), as Solomon who was dear to God was led astray by foreign wives.[49]

The reason for discouraging the Israelites from marrying members of other faiths was to prevent them from turning away from their God and worshipping other gods. They were concerned about the faithfulness of God's people. Discussing about interfaith marriage is not the main issue but is used to be a symbolic expression of the unfaithfulness of the Israelites to their God.[50]

New Testament

Positive aspects

In the New Testament there are evidences of people belonging to other faiths being married into the main stream of the chosen people. The genealogy of Jesus clearly shows that there are women from outside their faith coming into their families. Boaz', son of Salmon, born of Rahab was from a different tribe and later assimilated into the main stream of the Jewish people by marriage (Matt. 1:2-8). It is also pointed out that the wedding at Cana (Jn. 2:1-10) where Jesus was present was in the house of an alien.[51]

Paul also says, "If any believer has a wife who is an unbeliever and she consents to live with him, he should not divorce her. And if any woman has a husband who is an unbeliever and he consents to live with her, she should not divorce him. For the unbelieving husband is made holy through his wife and the unbelieving wife is made holy through her believing husband" (I Cor. 7:12-14). Paul is very clear that he is not disturbed by someone having an unbelieving husband or wife, but the important thing for him is the sanctity of family life. Paul guarantees that mixed marriages do not defile anybody. Even if one person remains an unbeliever the other should not ask for divorce. So, Paul sees a possibility of interfaith marriages.[52]

Negative aspects

II Corinthians 6: 14-7:1. "Do not be mismatched with unbelievers. For what partnership is there between righteousness and lawlessness? Or what fellowship is there between light and darkness? What agreement does Christ have with be liar?... therefore, come out from them, and be separate from them, says the Lord, and touch nothing unclean then I will welcome you..." (NRSV) This passage talks about the defilement of being together with the unbelievers.

This is a prohibition against *forming* close attachments with other faiths, using an agricultural metaphor about yoking (cf. Deut. 22:10; also Lev. 19:19). It clearly involved uncompromised with heathendom, such as contracting mixed marriages (cf. Deut. 7:1-3), initiating litigation before unbelievers in cases involving believers (1Co 6:1-8), or forming any relationship with unbelievers that would compromise Christian standards of Christian witness. Paul is content to state a general principle that needs specific application under the Spirit's guidance. The chief reason why believers must not enter any wrestle relationship with unbelievers (I Cor. 6.14a) is that they belong exclusively to God. Corporately they form "the temple of the living God" (cf. I Cor. 3:16-17; Eph 2:22; see also I Cor. 6:19). Paul's next quotation (Isa. 52:11) stresses God's demand for purity of life and separation from evil. In Isaiah, the call was for separation (or departure) from Babylon with its pagan idolatry. In Paul, the call is for separation from unbelievers with their pagan way of life.[53] Thus, all these passages reveal that, the Bible does not have a single approach to interfaith marriages. It was written and encouraged according to the situation of t context.

Marriage is a bond made together by males and females, to be together and to create wholeness. They need to become one, socially, religiously, politically and spiritually. However, from some of the interfaith married couples, we see that they are physically united, owning same belongings but not believing together. There are some couples who cannot come together religiously and spiritually. These seem that the marriage vows were not fully observed. Such marriages are increasing due to development of diverse culture and diverse religiosity. Such context led people to narrow down their fundamentalist ideology and allowed them to accept globally in wider aspects which seem no harm in marrying other religious person. No doubt, some couples settled well, some experienced hardships and difficult situations.

Endnotes

[1] Santhosh John, *Spirituality of Marriage* (New Delhi: ISPCK, 2011), 5. (Hereafter John, *Spirituality of Marriage*).

[2] Hazel W. Perkin, "Marriage" in *New International Bible Dictionary*, eds. J. D. Douglas, Merrill C. Tenney, (Grand Rapids, Michigan: Zondervan Publishing House, NY)

[3] R.K. Bower and G.K. Knapp, "Marriage," *The International Standard Bible Encyclopedia*, ed. Geoffray W. Briley, Volume Three K-P, (Grand Rapids: William B. Eerdmans Publishing Company, 1986), 261.

[4] John, *Spirituality of Marriage*, 6.

[5] C.N. Shankar Rao, *Sociology: Principles of Sociology with an Introduction to social thought* (Delhi: S. Chand and Company Pvt. Ltd, 2011), 327.

[6] Monte Neil Stewart, "Marriage Facts" http://www.law.harvard.edu (accessed 06 July 2015).

[7] Ezamo Murry, *An Introduction to Pastoral Care and Counseling* (New Delhi: ISPCK, 2009), 285. (Hereafter, Murry, *An Introduction to Pastoral Care and Counseling*).

[8] John, *Spirituality of Marriage*, 7.

[9] World Alliance of Reformed Churches, "Theology of marriage and the problems of mixed marriages", http://www.ecumenism.net (accessed 06 July 2015).

[10] Johann Christoph Arnold, "Sex, God and Marriage", http//: www.ntslibrary.com (accessed on 10/07/2015), 73.

[11] John, *Spirituality of Marriage*, 43.

[12] John, *Spirituality of Marriage*, 43.

[13] John, *Spirituality of Marriage*, 43.

[14] John, *Spirituality of Marriage*, 44.

[15] Migration Review Tribunal, "Mixed marriages in India", http://www.refworld.org (accessed 06 July 2015).

[16] Kyle Chapman, "Interfaith Marriage Counseling: Perspectives and Practices Among Christian Ministers" (M.A. Thesis, Graduate Faculty of Texas Tech University, 2011), 3. http://www.repositories.tdl.org (accessed on 16.10.2014).

[17] Immigration and Refugee Board of Canada, "India: Situation of inter-religious couples from both urban and rural locations, including societal attitudes, treatment by government authorities and the treatment of their children (2005-April 2012)," 11 May 2012, http://www.refworld.org (accessed 13 November 2014).

[18] Migration and Refugees Review Tribunal Country Advice, "Mixed Marriage in India", http://www.refworld.org (accessed on 22/10/ 2014).

[19] E. Nrio Ezung, *Socio-Cultural theology of marriage in Tribal Context* (Nagaland: Kyong Baptist Ekhumkho Sanrhyutsu, 2009), 27.

[20] (Exo. 20:17; 21:5; Lev. 18:8,11,14,15,16,20; 20:10; 21:13; Num.5:12; Deut. 5:21;22:22).

[21] Victor P. Hamilton, "Marriage" in *The Anchor Bible Dictionary*, Volume 4, edited by David Noel Freedman, Gary A. Herion eds., (New York: Doubleday publishing group, 1992), 565.

[22] Abraham married his half-sister (Gen. 20:12), Nahor married his niece Milcah (Gen. 11:29), Issac married his cousin Rebekah (Gen. 24:15), Esau married his cousin Mahalath (Gen.28:9) and Jacob married his cousin Rachel and Leah (Gen.29:12).

[23] Hamilton, "Marriage" in *The Anchor Bible Dictionary*, 563.

[24] Esau married two Hittites and a Canaanite (Gen.2634; 28:6-9), Joseph married an Egyptians (Gen.41:45), Judah to a Canaanite (Gen.28:21), Moses the Midianite (Exo. 2:21), Samson a Philistine (Judges 14), David a Chileab and Geshur (II Sam 3:3), Ahab Phoenician (I Kings 16:31), Solomon from many nations (I kings 11:1).

[25] Bathsheba married Uriah the Hittite (II Sam. 11:3), Esther married to the Persian King Ahasuerus. There is also the instance of Sheshan, who had only daughters, so he gave one of his daughters to his Egyptians slave (I Chro. 2:34-35).

[26] Hamilton, "Marriage" in *The Anchor Bible Dictionary*,564.

[27] J.S Wright, "marriage" in *New Bible Dictionary*, edited by J.D. Douglas, N. Hillyer eds., (Illinois: Intervarsity press, 2003), 735.

[28] Hagar select a wife for her son Ishmael from Egypt (Gen. 21:21), Sarah select a wife for Isaac (Gen. 25:20), the choice of Rebekah is the classic case of parental arranged marriages. Isaac plays no role other than finding the choice to his satisfaction (Gen. 24:7), Jacob select a girl for his son Er (Gen. 38:6).

[29] Hamilton, "Marriage" in *The Anchor Bible Dictionary*,565.

[30] Shimprui Khuiso, "The elopement and its impact on the Tangkhul Naga society: A Christian Education perspective" (M.Th. Thesis Eastern Theological College, Jorhat, 2015), 41.

[31] Emmanuel E. James, "*Ethics: A Biblical perspective*" (Bangalore: Theological Book Trust, 2001), 305.

[32] John, *Spirituality of marriage*, 52.

[33] John Macarthur, *The divorce dilemma: God's last word on lasting commitment* (Maharashtra: Grace to India, 2009), 39.

[34] John, *Spirituality of marriage*, 53.

[35] Macarthur, *The divorce dilemma: God's last word on lasting commitment*, 11.

[36] John, *Spirituality of marriage*, 53.

[37] David Instone Brewer, *Divorce and remarriage in the Bible: The social and literary context* (Grand Rapids: William Eerdmans Publishing Company, 2002), 2.

[38] Howard J. Clinebell and Charlotte H. Clinebell, *The intimate Marriage* (New York: Harper and Row Publishers, 1970), 19.

[39] William F. Luck, *Divorce and Remarriage: Recovering the Biblical view* (San Francisco: Harper and Row Publisher, 1987), 45.

[40] John, *Spirituality of marriage*, 53.

[41] J. Russell Chandran, *Christian Ethics* (New Delhi: ISPCK,2011), 111.

[42] John, *Spirituality of marriage*, 56.

[43] John, *Spirituality of marriage*, 55.

[44] "History of Jewish interfaith marriage", www. Interfaithfamily.com (accessed on 22.06.1015).

[45] L.E. Sahanam, *belonging but not Believing: Interfaith marriage* (New Delhi: ISPCK, 2009), 23. (Hereafter, Sahanam, *belonging but not Believing: Interfaith marriage*).

[46] Sahanam, *Belonging but not Believing: Interfaith marriage*, 23.

[47] Sahanam, *Belonging but not Believing: Interfaith marriage*, 21.

[48] William Smith, "Marriage" in *Smith's Bible Dictionary*, eds. Francis and Mary Peloubet (Chattanooge: AMG Publishers, 2008), 388.

[49] Sahanam, *Belonging but not Believing: Interfaith marriage*, 22.

[50] Sahanam, *Belonging but not Believing: Interfaith marriage*, 22.

[51] Sahanam, *Belonging but not Believing: Interfaith marriage*, 24.

[52] Sahanam, *Belonging but not Believing: Interfaith marriage*, 24.

[53] Kenneth L. Barker & John Kohlenberger, *Zondervan NIV Bible Commentary* (Grand Rapids, Michigan, Zondervan Publishing House, NY).

CHAPTER - 2

Critical Overview of Interfaith Marriage

Every issue has its own valid reasons, so also, interfaith marriages have their own causes. We have seen that; such marriages have been practicing since the Old Testament times, but it was rare. Consequently, when we see in contemporary situation, such marriages upsurge rapidly. To discuss deeper about the issues of interfaith marriage, it is right process to begin with the causes of how it happens. Moreover, in every issue there is always an impact either positive or negative. However, in this book as it deals on the issues from negative perspectives, the impact will focus only on negative aspects covering various areas.

Causes of interfaith-marriage

Why have the interfaith marriages increased and become such a pressing issue? Interfaith married couples can be found throughout the world.

Misconception

Many youths have a wrong concept towards their partner. In the context of Manipur, most of the Christians live in hilly areas and the Hindus in the valley. Some Christian women believed that they will not work in the field or become cultivators when they marry a Hindu who are in the valley with higher per-capita income. On the other hand, the Hindu boys think that they will lighten the work if they marry Christian women because they are hard working people. Thus, with this misconception they come together under one-fold and hence interfaith marriage is ubiquitous.

Love affairs

People often meet their partners while studying or at work.. Although a student's status and life experiences during academic period are normally marked by a transient, they also tend to contribute and give their hearts to one another, thereby developing relationship by sharing different life experiences. Thus, they choose or accept a lover without deep reconsideration. When the relationship gets deeper, it is difficult to break or annul the relationship. Most of the youngsters developed infatuation without deep thought and without parents' concern. Therefore, sometimes by no means though both the lovers belong to different religion, they decided to go for settlement.[1]

Children's education in mixed culture

Children's education in a mixed national background is also one of the causes to develop the ideology of interfaith marriage. Such children have bilingual capabilities and habituated with a bi-cultural environment. Thus, for such children there are difficulties in differentiating cultural variation and religious differences and as such they are considered as one and have the sentiment of equality of all culture and religion. They develop a sense of national assimilation that obviously subsumes the creation of a bi-cultural project to that of the present lifestyle. Children's upbringing in a mixed cultural environment will turn out as an experience of peripatetic living.[2] They lived and are raised up together in same schools, colleges, sports clubs and jobs. Therefore, the physical proximity has led to social contact and has quickly developed into sexual attraction and emotional bonds. It is because in the beginning they know each other only by their looks and profession and not by their different faith.[3]

Not raising children in Godly way

Parents have huge responsibility to bring up children in proper ways. The greatest pride of any parents are well brought up children and the greatest sorrow are wayward children. Children who are raise up in godly discipline will be properly equipped to face the cruel and difficult world and will be shielded and protected from wrong influences. These children will never run away from God's sight. But those children who are not raised in God's way will not able to overcome when temptation and difficulty appears. Their faith will be shaken and so they will not maintain the sanctity of their life..[4]

Changes into wider society

The changes of the society's attitude towards interfaith marriages from narrow to wider aspects became one of the causes for the growth of interfaith marriage. Most important of all is the transformation of society from one that was strictly divided into groups and which judged people by the category to which they belonged to a society that valued the principles of egalitarianism and treated people as individuals. What do you do? Has superseded to what do you believe? Which was the key question when meeting someone new, especially of the opposite sex? The negative attitude towards other faith that had in the past has changed, so now interfaith marriages do not become a hard or crucial issue. The religious pluralism that exists now has helped people and makes faith appear to lack objective truth in the eyes of many and to be a subjective matter.[5]

Increases of diverse group relationship

In diverse societies, one's likelihood of residing within homogenous groups is low. However, the expansion of a group increases the number of choices an individual may have in mate selection within that group. Not only two groups become more similar through repeated interaction with other groups, but group expansion allows for similarities between groups to grow while the differences between groups become less influential. As group grows, they begin to share common characteristics with other groups, and because the groups share commonalities they become less distinct from one another. The narrower the circle they commit to the less freedom of individuality they possess. Therefore, the relevance of one's individual identity associated with a religious group decreases, and as a result the available number of possible mates increases. There are many people who identify themselves as religious people but are not intimately connected with one religious group alone. This provides closer association with other religious groups and allow for some to select a mate partner from other religious groups.[6]

Social media

Social media brings lots of changes in terms of development, knowledge and day to day lifestyles. Social media makes it easier to let people know one another. In short, it makes the world smaller. With the help of social networking sites such as, my space and Facebook, many people got the opportunity to connect with different people to come together and hang out together. It provides opportunities to express one's feeling openly and personally. It also provides the sources to seek future inmates through the sites like shadi.com. Many people were influenced and they were married with the help of this site. People sometimes promised to be one's spouse without knowing personally but through phone calls. Due to this influence by social media people failed to think critically about someone's personality, moral values, religious rights and parents' wishes. Thus, social media give chances to let people from different faiths to go for marriage (settlement).[7]

Accidental and unintentional

There are many individuals who did not enter interfaith marriage knowingly or for any reasons, but it just happened that way. For many people, marrying other faith are not just unintentional but also against their own principles. In some cases, people go for this marriage due to pregnancy outside of the wedlock.[8] In some incident, daughters are taken forcefully by money lender when the father cannot repay the debts. It was unexpected and was totally against the will of the daughter. Sometimes parents prearranged the marriage programme for their daughter to different religious person by taking bribe without the knowledge of their daughter. No doubt, marriages also occur when a man from other faith saved a girl from unexpected danger like communal violence, religious violence etc.

Search for better life

Many people are in search of better economic life. Some people leave their native village and goes to the cities in search of job and better opportunity. Majority of people who are in rural villages survive through cultivation. It requires hard working to meet minimum ends such as two square meals a day. Mostly they do work throughout the year (cultivation) to maintain their livelihood. There is no way to live a luxurious life in that situation. Thus, whoever goes to mainland cities hardly contemplate returning to their native village for future settlement. They even seek for their inmates' partners within themselves (those who live in cities). Sometimes, they tend to search even from other faith. In some cases, people choose to marry from other faith and live a better life instead of marrying from the same religion and live a worse life. At this juncture, religion or faith is not the main concern of settlement but better future prospect rather becomes more important concern for settlement.

Effects and problems of interfaith-marriage

Statistics prove that a high percentage of interfaith marriages have lost the fervor of their faith and that only a small percentage of them provide their children with religious education. Hence, religious indifference of both the parties is the main threat of such marriages.[9] Interfaith couples can experience opposition from parents, friends or religious communities. There are many things to consider, particularly regarding the upbringing and religious education of children and any potential pressure that might come from within the marriage, from the families of the partners, or from their respective religious communities to convert to other religion.[10]

Psychological problems

Anxiety disorder

As the term suggests, anxiety disorders are those in which unrealistic, irrational fear of disabling intensity is present. They experience severe psychological traumas like a life-threatening situation, witnessing physical violence, becoming the victim of physical and emotional violence. Thus, it develops post-traumatic stress disorders.[11] Family members have, in turn, threatened couples, filed false cases of abduction against couples, or killed spouses as a way of upholding the family's honor.[12]Anxiety, apprehension, chronic tension, insomnia, repetitive nightmares, feelings of depression, inability to relax, withdrawal from social contacts and suicidal tendencies will also develop. All these unusual experiences even lead to panic disorder resulting to shortness of breath, dizziness and fear of dying. At last, this kind of abnormal disorder affects in the relationship of couples and with the parents.[13]

Phobic disorders

A phobic is a persistent fear of some objects or situation that presents no actual danger to the person or in which the danger is magnified out of proportion to its seriousness. Some phobias involve an exaggerated fear of things that most people fear such as darkness, fire and snakes. Some phobias are fear of big crowds, stand in front of people. Social Phobia also known as social anxiety disorder, which is characterized by persistent, irrational fear generally linked to the presence of other people (fear of public speaking) develops and this give hindrances in their day to day life. This phobia is maintained in part by secondary gains, such as increased attention, sympathy, over controlled by other, receives constant threatened and experienced excessive fear.[14]

Obsessive Compulsive Disorder (OCD)

An obsession is a persistent preoccupation with something typically of an idea or a feeling. A compulsion is an impulsive experienced as irresistible. Individual with obsessive Compulsive Disorders feel compelled to think about something that they do not want to think about or to carry out some action against their will. Some persons in such marriage are forced to think and act in a certain way against their will for which they have no control. They were asked to leave their interest, desire, feelings, faith and forced to adopt new things without realizing their interest and concern.

These behaviors can be distressing to the person interfering with his/her occupational or social functioning. These individuals have a personality characterized by feeling of inadequacy and insecurity, a tendency toward feelings of guilt and high vulnerability to threat. They are chronically over aroused and unable to relax. Such obsessive-compulsive behaviors occur in the point of facing stressors that reduces the toleration and coping levels of the individuals. Thus, psychologically they were affected by the Obsessive-Compulsive Disorder.[15]

Guilt with major depression

The couples of inter-faith marriage mostly experienced opposition from in-laws which develop a sense of conflict, bitterness and misunderstanding, with damaging and long-lasting consequences for those relationships. This hostility provokes enormous guilt for the couples and this guilt makes the task of emotional separation more difficult to achieve.[16] Some persons experienced victimization, neglected by the parents, declining interest, and develops the sense of isolation and hopelessness which ultimately leads to depression. They are marked by sadness and insomniac character and do not have any pleasure to do things sincerely. This diminished all their talents because they are forced to leave their interest, diminished even in cognitive capacities, and instead of mingling with society it develops sense of inferiority. This depression affects badly in human day today works. Sometimes there is also noted the suicidal tendency.[17]

Inferiority complex

In some cases, a spouse's (who came from other faith) view are never accepted, never recognized as important and never consider its contribution as beneficial. Moreover, he/she was mostly threatened and regarded as inferior person; he/she is never regarded as important and worthy person. Thus, those people automatically developed inferiority complex. Such person is characterized by the feelings of incompetency and the lack of personal adequacy. Being a human, every person tends to think themselves as important person who possess a unique quality. Every person has a sense of comparison which make themselves proud when he/she finds themselves better than other person. This inferiority complex drives the person to thinks as unfit, unworthy person who cannot do any good works and who is good for nothing.[18]

Fear of future

Fear can come in response to a variety of situations. Different people are afraid of failure, the future, achieving success, rejection intimacy, conflict, meaninglessness in life, sickness, death, loneliness and a host of other real or imagined possibilities. Spouse of interfaith marriage develops fear especially for their future because their works are mostly rejected which always make them failure. Thus, they always think that there is no value of living on this earth. Their thought is occupied by a sense of hopelessness which has no capacity or skill to do any good things or to do good works for the development of the family and of the society.[19]

Sociological problems

Cross cultural problems

The partners coming from different religious background have cultural difference too. Thus, they have cross cultural adjustment issue. The boundary and the limitation of their lifestyle set by the parents may be different. One might come from an independent cultural lifestyle and the other might be from the interdependent culture. Thus, they need to negotiate such matter and need to navigate this cross-cultural issue by openly discussing differences and trying to learn about each partner's culture.[20] As per Hindu and Muslim culture, taking beef and pork is prohibited whereas for Christians they enjoy eating those red meat. Words and actions are always related to the culture in one way or the other. Thus, this are reflected even in their mind and thought of development. The art of compromising is valuable, but this involve painful choices because it needs to give up certain habits and letting go of some expectations in return for one's partner and relinquishing some of their preconceptions.[21]

Social reservations

The parties of an interfaith marriage are frowned upon and are not warmly welcomed by people on almost all occasions. So, although marriage is a personal matter, it is the society where the couples do live and socialize. Therefore, they must conform to its norms. Consequently, social approval or disapproval has significant impact upon a couple's life. If the interfaith marriage parties are not economically independent, their social lives may be particularly precarious. This social unacceptance has its roots again in the religious disapproval of such marriages.[22]

Impact of extended family

The couples of interfaith marriages may encounter negative pressure from their families and possibly from their respective religious organizations. The partner who lacks his or her partners' family acceptance can be negatively impacted. He or she may have a decreased sense of well being and feel like an outsider. This can cause discord between the couple. Covert alliances between a partner and his or her family that is not accepting of the partner can negatively impact the relationship and inhibit future marital happiness.[23]

Societal rejection

Most societies do not want to accept or recognized willingly the spouse of interfaith marriage. This is because it affects the society one way or the other. When there is problem within the family this insidiously affects even the society. The spouse of interfaith may sometimes have different purpose of marrying other faith. There are instances of interfaith spouse becoming a spy or becoming destructive force. Moreover, in terms of administrating the society, there will be an absence in communication matter, in contribution and in terms of living harmonious lives. Thus, most of the societies refrained them from recognition and do not want them to communicate freely from deep and serious matter. The societies never give them full authority to take care of the society because they have the sense of suspiciousness and distrust.

Loneliness

Loneliness is a painful consciousness that lack meaningful contact with others. It involves a feeling of inner emptiness which can be accompanied by sadness, discouragement, sense of isolation, restlessness, anxiety and an intense desire to be wanted and needed by someone. Many people often feel "left out," unwanted, or rejected even when they are surrounded by others. Loneliness involves the lack or loss of intimate relationship with another person or persons. It is the feeling of aimlessness, anxiety and emptiness. The person feels that he/she is "out of it" and on the margin of it. The spouse of interfaith marriage experience loneliness because most society rejects them, unwilling to socialize with them, even the rejection from friends. These people yearn to have someone to be with them whom they can share their feeling and needs.[24]

Intra personal problems

Weakness in building relationship

Among the couples of interfaith marriage, the task of achieving intimacy is even more daunting since there are many activities that take for granted when a person grows up in different types of home or community. There are many nonverbal gesture and facial expressions, the idiomatic sayings and the types of foods and holiday celebrations that characterize a cultural experience. There are also the symbols of the different faiths such as the Cross and Trisul which often evoke powerful emotional responses in people. When people of one faith and cultural background understands and identify the other then it helps to build intimacy. When two people from different backgrounds and faith comes together, there is a lack of commonness. The opportunities for misunderstanding, confusion and hurting are plentiful.[25]

God's purposes of sex in marriage are procreation (Gen. 1:27-28), pleasure (Deut.24:5) and protection (I Cor. 7:1-2). Failure to sexually satisfy each other in marriage may lead to a spouse looking outside the marriage for fulfillment.[26] Sex and love are commonly associated together. Love needs sex and sex needs love. Many couples have sexual problems due to loss of sexual desire. And the cause was by the breakdown of the personal relationship between the couple.[27] Since the couples of interfaith marriages experienced physical harassment and verbal assault, this resulted to diminishing intimacy and widening the gap of love. Eventually the effects of love effect even in sexual relationship where couples cannot have healthy sexual relationship.

Lost human's lives

There was a case in Punjab where a Sikh woman and a Hindu man were attacked by the woman's parents because of interfaith marriage as well as a case from Hyderabad in which the parents of a Hindu woman repeatedly tried to kill her and her Muslim husband. *The Hindustan Times* reports on a case in which a 24-year-old woman from Kinawli village in Shahpur, Thane district, was beaten to death by family members for secretly marrying and converting to Buddhism (14 Apr. 2011). The police arrested and charged her father, brother and two sisters with murder (*The Hindustan Times* 14 Apr. 2011). The Chandigarh-based multi-media company Day and Night News reports a case in which a man accused his in-laws of killing his wife because they were in an inter-religious marriage (26 Feb. 2012).[28]

According to The *Globe and Mail* article, in November 2011 in Uttar Pradesh, the father and two brothers of a 21-year-old woman were charged with shooting and killing her because she was in a relationship with a man of a different religion (7th Dec. 2011). An article in *Indian Currents*, a Delhi-based weekly English magazine, states that Muslim boys in Karnataka state have been attacked for speaking with Hindu girls and accused of trying to convert them through marriage (15th Feb. 2012). The US *International Religious Freedom Report 2009* provides details of such attacks in 2009, noting that "Hindu extremists" assaulted Muslim boys talking to Hindu girls, often on public transportation, in the Dakshina Kannada and Udupi districts of Karnataka (26th Oct. 2009).[29]

Divorce

Interfaith marriage couples have marginally higher rate of divorce than the same faith marriage couples. According to the findings of research, the higher rate of divorce in these couples are because of facing extra compromises and accepting difficult and unwilling decisions. A person who is prepared to flout their parents' wishes in the choice of marriage partner may also be more liable to resist the compromises necessary for a harmonious relationship. A day to day basic need is a security for humans and if one marriage partner is often presenting challenges in terms of emotional expectations, family roles and in ways of communicating, then this can be unsettling and can lead to the collapse of trust. Most of the interfaith marriage couples are opposed by families, relatives and even the community. Thus, they hardly receive any help or support from the family making them lonely and insecure. Loneliness and insecurity led to change their mind and interest especially when they faced trouble and difficulties. Hence, at last divorce mostly became the last solution.[30]

Problems with in-laws

In the beginning all seems to be well because the in-laws can control, adjust and bear one's differences. Daughter in-law can surrender her own desire and submit to follow and accept her in-laws' will. However, as time passes, and the family becomes larger, it becomes difficult for the daughter in-law to be submissive always and give attention to the in-laws. As the environments of raising up their lives was different their expectations and characteristics mostly differ. Sometimes such differences create divisions in the family between the in-laws (including husband). At this juncture, husbands have a hard time negotiating with their parents because if he sides with the wife his parents' relationship will be widened and if he sides to parents then the wife's relationship will be weakened. Many bitter relationships among the in-laws seem to be created due to the ideology of confrontation, mutual distrust and the competitive spirit.[31]

Cross transactions

An immediate consequence of bitter relationship and different ideology leads to the sense of uncontrolled over one's body and decision making. When the relationships with their spouse's parents and in-laws are not healthy, the spouse of interfaith marriage may find it very difficult to handle because they cannot identify whom to blame. Once the relationship between in-laws is weakened and worsens then it obtains and develops an attitude of negativity. The work done, and the words spoken always receives inconsistent and receives unexpected response. Thus, the communications are impaired, and the individual feels misunderstood, hurt or angered. The gestures, facial expressions, body posture, voice tone and vocabulary used will always be in negative aspects and unpleasant acts.[32]

Problems related to children

Selection of children

According to the culture of Hinduism, higher preference is given to a male child rather than female child. This is because of dowry system and of the inheritance. Thus, they continue to have children till they give birth to a male child. In case of inheritance everybody prefers male child because they are the rightful heir. However, for most of the Christians, they do not have strict culture and policy that prefer male child over female child. They believe and consider all children are equal and are the gift and blessing from God. Thus, there is no difference in accepting a male or a female child. Most of the Hindu families do not warmly welcome the female child and so their attitude really affects the child in her holistic development. It develops depression and stress, and this leads to the self attempt of life (suicide). All children expect equal treatment, concern and love from parents but spouses from different faith hardly do so due to differences in desire and preferences.

Confusion in raising children

Couples of interfaith marriage experience confusion in raising children. All parents have a sacred responsibility for the spiritual upbringing of their children, but interfaith couples have a double important responsibility because of the possibility of causing religious confusion in their children's lives. If adults can feel the confusion of following multi-religion, then children will be affected more when two religions pull them. Some children of interfaith parents experience overwhelming sadness because they are not like the other children whose parents share the same faith. Some children in interfaith homes do not want to be a part of any religion when they grow older because of the conflict feelings they experienced while growing up.[33] Children having a dual religious identity with religious education in both faiths result in being exposed to both traditions. But, children who accept a dual identity as natural are often confused of who they really are. On the contrary, children having no religious identity and no religious education live a neutral life and have a high probability of becoming an agnostic or an atheist.[34]

Effect on faith identity or lives of children

The religious identity of children is often an important and highly emotive part of the negotiation that takes place between interfaith couples. Children of such marriages attend both the Church and temple/*Mandir*/Mosque fellowships. They learn about the heritage of both their parents and can decide for themselves which often leads to confusion in religious affiliation when they are adults. There have been several commentators who have stated that the mental health and well being of children depend upon having a clear religious and ethnic identity. In addition, the practice of religion has been found to help children avoid the influences of drugs, alcohol and adolescent sexual relations. According to research, it also shows that children whose parents were firm, consistent, involved and affectionate did best in school and in their relationships later in life.[35] Religious identity is the way in which they perceive themselves and how others label them. It is because they will require in all stages of life, ranging from nursery to school friends (I am Christian/Hindu/Muslims. What are you?) and to fill a form either in Hospital or for a job, identity of the religion is always required (religion of the patient).[36]

Headache in children's wedding

When the children grows and their wedding approaches it becomes even more problematic for parents. The practical matters such as how the wedding should be celebrated are a crucial and important issue to be taken up and must be treated carefully and sensitively; for example, to have the wedding outside the church. An interfaith marriage needs proper and appropriate preparation, strong and skilled support, as well as pastoral care at every stage of the couple's life together.[37] Children who are raised with both religious identities are confused with which religious traditions they should associate but children who are raised with only one religious identity can decide which religious tradition to be followed. Children with no religious identity do not bother and will never follow any religious traditions for tying the knot. They may simply choose to elope which affects the prestige of their parents.

Problems related to religious affair

Wedding ceremony

There is also a problem in the wedding ceremony to be performed when they are of different faiths. It is because every religion has its own religious functions to be performed during marriage ceremony. Some of the problematic queries are will the wedding be of religious or secular ceremony? Whose priest or religious leaders will be administering the wedding? In which religious procedure will the wedding ceremony be performed? What rituals and customs will be incorporated into the ceremony itself? Sometimes, the ceremony decisions are fraught with anxiety for the wedding couple, because the desire and wishes of parents varies from family to family. The wedding simply cannot be done in the favor of one's family alone because it will affect in building future relationship. Favoritism to one family also creates tremendous resentment from the other family members whose religious tradition has been ignored or purposefully excluded.[38]

Losing one's faith

Interfaith marriage leads to a secularization of religious commitment and identity (religious identity). It faces adversity in negotiation for marriage and receives severe social disapproval. In some cases, one partner must surrender or lose their faith to live together as a couple.[39] King Solomon had interfaith marriages from different faiths and with many foreign women such as an Egyptian, Moabite, Ammonite, Edomite, Sidonian and Hittite women. As a result, in the end his spirit turned away from God to other gods and no longer became true to the Lord his God. Thus, he did what is evil in the sight of the Lord and did not completely follow the Lord. (I Kings 11:1-8)

Problems in decision making

When the family takes decisions in matters of moral, ethical and religious issues like contraception, abortion and even about the future of the children, the couple face a lot of difficulties. Married couples face challenges even when both spouses share the same convictions in the religious and moral spheres of life. It is because of their differences in religious teaching and faith.[40] Camilla a Catholic woman who married a Sikh man describes the difficulties in making decisions in relation to contraception. She and her Sikh husband wanted to have children, but not immediately, and she had no objections to the idea of family planning. However, she felt that she did not want to be the one taking the contraceptives or the pill because Christian teachings consider such action as sin. Therefore, she preferred her husband to wear protection to which he objected because the pleasure in intercourse is not exciting.[41] All these matters always reflect or are related to the religious affairs in one way or the other. Dedication and the naming of the child also is another serious issue pursued by interfaith couples.

Victims in religious sphere

It will be difficult for couples of interfaith marriages to become an active member of any church (however, they can be associate members). Hence, when it comes to delegating the responsibility they always become the victims. The attitudes of religious leaders (both Hindus and Christianity) towards those couples are different from other. They will not be visited often and are not free to express willingly as the religious leaders themselves hesitate to talk and give counsel due to matters of different faith and belief. So even the couples are deterred from receiving counseling from clergy members. Religious leaders hardly had any contact with them thinking that it will be of no value. This lack of confidence shown by religious leaders towards those marriage couple is unpleasant for both the couple as well as the religion.[42]

Thus, interfaith marriages are happening and increasing due to misconception of one's life, love affairs irrespective of diverse religions sending children in mixed culture for education. t increase of diverse group relationship, advancements of social media and technologies and sometimes by accidental and unintentional while in search of better life. This kind of marriage leads to various kinds of psychological problems particularly due to differences in understanding and feelings. Such married couples face difficulties in adjustment with society due to cross cultural differences. They even experience intra personal problems because of disagreement and inequality. After bearing children they had hard time particularly in parenting and even in religious set up they mostly had a second-class treatment from both the religious leaders.

Endnotes

[1] Sofia Gasper, "Mixed marriages between European free movers", http//www.cles.iscte.pt. (accessed on 24/06/2015)

[2] Gasper, "Mixed marriages between…", http//www.cles.iscte.pt. (accessed on 24/06/2015)

[3] Jonathan Romain, "The Effects of Mixed-Faith Marriages on Family Life and Identity", http//www.anthro.ox.aca (accessed on 24/06/15).

[4] Juliet Thomas, *Raising Children God's way* (Secunderabad: OM Books, 2002), 7.

[5] Romain, "The Effects of Mixed-Faith Marriages…," http//www.anthro. ox.aca, 278.

[6] Chapman, "Interfaith Marriage Counseling…" http://www.repositories. tdl.org, 12,13.

[7] Anna Leon Guerrero, *Social problems: community, policy and social action* (New Delhi: SAGE Publications, 2009), 259.

[8] Naasiha Abrahams, "Managing socio-religious expectations in an intimate space: Examining Muslim interfaith marriage amongst working class communities in Cape Town (Master of Social Science in Religious Studies Thesis, Faculty of the Humanities University of Cape Town, 2012), http// www.open.uct.ac.za (accessed on 22/06/ 2015).

[9] John, *Spirituality of Marriage*, 94.

[10] Bishop conference of Indian and Wales, http://www.googles.com (accessed on 22/06/ 2015).

[11] John, *Spirituality of Marriage*, 71.

[12] Immigration and Refugee Board of Canada, "India: Situation of inter-religious couples from both urban and rural locations…," http://www.refworld. org (accessed 13 November 2014).

[13] John, *Spirituality of Marriage*, 72.

[14] L.Wright, "Anxiety disorders" in *Dictionary of Pastoral care and counseling*, edited by Rodney J. Hunter, Nancy J. Ramsey (Bangalore: Theological Publication of India, 2007),49.

[15] John, *Spirituality of Marriage*, 73.

[16] Allan Schwartz, "The emotional challenges of interfaith marriage", http://www.googles.com (accessed on 22/10/ 2014).

[17] John, *Spirituality of Marriage*, 76.

[18] Rebecca Sumi, "A study on the psychological problems of widows in Sumi community: Implication for pastoral Care and counseling" (M.Th. Thesis, Clark Theological College, Mokokchung, 2015), 7. (Hereafter, Sumi, "A study on the psychological problems of widows in Sumi community...").

[19] Sumi, "A study on the psychological problems of widows in Sumi community...", 8.

[20] "Cross-Cultural navigation", http://www.googles.com (accessed on 22/10/ 2014).

[21] Romain, "The Effects of Mixed-Faith Marriages...", http//www.anthro. ox.aca.

[22] Mohammad Moin Uddin, "Inter-religious Marriage in Bangladesh: An Analysis of the Existing Legal Framework", The Chittagong University Journal of Law, Vol. XIII, 2008, p.117- 139. http://www.googles.com (accessed on 22/06/ 2015).

[23] Tammy J. Shaffer, "Interfaith Marriage and Counseling Implications," http:www.citeseerx.ist.psu.edu (accessed on 22/10/ 2014).

[24] Gary R. Collins, *Christian Counseling: A Comprehensive Guide* (Texas: Word Books, 1980), 72-73.

[25] Schwartz, "The emotional challenges of interfaith marriage", http://www.googles.com.

[26] Dennis Rainey, *Preparing for marriage* (California: Gospel Light publishing house, 1977), 217.

[27] Imtijungla Jamir, *Restore our family* (Nagaland: Disciples Bible College, 2006), 79.

[28]Immigration and Refugee Board of Canada, "India: Situation of inter-religious couples from both urban and rural locations...," http://www.refworld. org (accessed 13 November 2014).

[29] Immigration and Refugee Board of Canada, "India: Situation of inter-religious couples from both urban and rural locations...," http://www.refworld. org (accessed 13 November 2014).

[30] Romain, "The Effects of Mixed-Faith Marriages", http//www.anthro. ox.aca, 291.

[31] John, *Spirituality of Marriage*, 106.

[32] J.C. Landrud, "Transactionl analysis" in Dictionary *of Pastoral care and counseling,* edited by Rodney J. Hunter, Nancy J. Ransey eds., (Bangalore: Theological Publications of India, 2007), 1285.

[33] Elisha Hope Terre, "Interfaith marriage and its effects on the family: A Jewish perspective" (M.Sc. Thesis, The Graduate Faculty University of Wisconsin-Platteville, 2012), http://www.googles.com (accessed on 22/10/ 2014).

[34] Romain, "The Effects of Mixed-Faith Marriages…", http//www.anthro. ox.aca, 289.

[35] Schwartz, "The emotional challenges of interfaith marriage", http://www. googles.com.

[36] Romain, "The Effects of Mixed-Faith Marriages…", http//www.anthro. ox.aca, 288.

[37] Bishop conference of Indian and Wales, http://www.googles.com (accessed on 22/06/ 2015).

[38] Steven Carr Reuben, *"There's an egg on your Seder plate,"* (West Port: Praeger publisher, 2008), 28. (Hereafter, Reuben, *"There's an egg on your Seder plate*).

[39] Abrahams, "Managing socio-religious expectations in an intimate…," http//www.open.uct.ac.za.

[40] John, *Spirituality of Marriage*, 94.

[41] Romain, "The Effects of Mixed-Faith Marriages…," http//www.anthro. ox.aca.

[42] Chapman, "Interfaith Marriage Counseling…" 53. http://www.repositories. tdl.org.

CHAPTER - 3

Scenario and Predicament of Interfaith Marriage

This chapter attempts to analyze the experiences and the difficulties in relation to the psychological and social life of interfaith married couples as well as the difficulties in parenting their children. The psychological challenges are connected to the daily problems and they are linked with the social challenges resulting from moral pressure which impact the parenting issues. The purpose of undertaking this chapter is to examine whether there will be significant psychological problems, social problems and parenting issues among couples of interfaith marriages and to encourage and stimulate them by giving advice and response from Pastoral care and counseling perspective for a better and healthier life.

This interfaith marriage has been existing since long decades back but it was very rare. In the past, there was not close relation with different religious people. There was a huge gap between the hilly people (tribal) and the valley people (non-tribal). As per the history, the non-tribal considered tribal as unclean. So, tribal are forbidden to enter in the house of non-tribal not even in their household area. Their relationship in those days is almost similar with that of Hindu high caste and the outcaste. Such bitter interconnection makes the relationship unhealthy and creates huge distance between these two groups. However, as the time passed by and development takes places with the passage of time, even people's sentiment started changing from negative to positive. They realize that unless they work together by joining hands, by building deep rapport, by sharing views together, and by educating equally it is not possible to bring advancement. Thus, this became one of the turning points to let the tribal and non-tribal work closely without any prejudices and feelings. Consequently, children from both groups study together in the same educational institutions become friends, sometimes even closer than family. Therefore, the feelings of sanctity group and the unclean group is vanishing and adopting the attitude of oneness . This results in the excessive census of interfaith marriage couples in the present days, especially among the youngsters.

Majority of the interfaith couples marry at the early age (16-25), which are under the group of later adolescence to early young adulthood. In this stage, children are struggling for their identity, seeking the goal, purpose and the meaning of their life. In the process of searching, when relationship interrupts it brings confusion and compels to take hasty decision. Normally, it is a grade where children want to stray away from parent, dependent to independent. They wish to escape away from parental control and decide to live as per their aspiration which they feel as the absolute. Thus, their discerning power, decision making ability is weak and unable to think for long term (future). In this juncture, youths start developing love affairs within opposite sex. They enjoy to be with friends and they try things to make themselves to be attracted by the opposite sex. Although, they experience love, those who have found their purpose of living will never take prompt decision specially to get married at this young age. But those who are confused of their future sees nothing and thus take abrupt agreement which is immature opinion. Therefore, mostly such marriage happened out of ignorance and unstable understanding.

Looking at the status of their occupation, few couples are employed, and they run businesses by profession, but majority are just mere cultivator/farmer, who doesn't have prospered future aspect. In one sense, they became mere cultivator because they get married before the completion of their studies. They are cultivator because they are uneducated and they get married at the very early age because they worry for their future as there is no prospects to prolong their life as bachelor. As per the mentality of the context, uneducated bachelors have more disadvantages when they enter adulthood. These practices sometimes force them to choose their life partners early. On the other side, if they are too young either the government or the private sector will not employ them. When they are vocationally unfit, it is not possible to get a job. The job always required some abilities. The companies or the employers are always looking forward to finding persons who have the ability, degree, experience and interest. Their early age at marriage disallow them high degree with ability and sharp aptitude. Thus, as a result it makes them jobless.

The impact of culture always attaches with the religious affiliation. Since, it is a patriarchal culture, the tradition believes and expects that a female should follow the male's culture and religion. Simultaneously, it happened to many couples particularly a female. Though she professes other religion, after marriage she obviously joins together with husband. In fact, there are also some female who remains in her own faith and religion. Surprisingly, there are also another group of couples who acted out unexpectedly. Before marriage they are so active in religious work but after marriage because of their spouse's religion they live as atheist, without affiliating with any religion. They neither remain in their former religion nor accept their spouse religion. But, as mentioned above majority of the female changes their religion to husband's religion after marriage.

Psychological problems

It is the effect on mental and emotional dysfunction which leads to think negatively. Whoever has this kind of problems will live with tension and stress as they will hardly find peace and good rest. Indeed, the psychological problems are part of everyone's life. Yet, some lives are afflicted by these conditions far more overwhelmingly and painfully than others. However, this can be mitigated through the expenditure of considerable personal effort and often with the help of a counselor required. It would be unrealistic and undesirable to expect or attempt to eradicate them from one's life permanently. Yet one can provide skills to handle oneself carefully for betterment. Some of the psychological problems are discussed below:

I feel that I am not the right person for my partner

Each spouse of the interfaith marriage has different feelings, experiences and opinions in relation to their daily life such as in creating intimate relationship with the spouse and its family. Some couples, after marriage, realizes that they are not the right person for their spouse or they are not made for each other as they don't have similar perception and understanding.[1] Their interest and concept always differ thus it results in undesired atmosphere. Earlier before marriage they both had misconception about the partners but when it was not fulfilled their interest withdraw away. If they withdraw their feelings, egoism develops, and it affects in transactional process. It impacted in their life position, 'I'm ok you are not ok,' where self is viewed as effective (I'm ok) but others as ineffective (you are not ok). They will not give much respect for others and easily find fault on others. When a person is ruled over other that is not a right principle and if principle is not right there will be no happy life.[2]

I do not feel comfortable with my spouse's parents

There are couples who don't feel comfortable with the in-laws.[3] Definitely, it will be because the background and lifestyle are purely opposite. The present life is a result of the past and naturally it is very hard to transform once it is instilled in one's heart. One is from tribal set up, brought up in a hilly area whereas the other is from non-tribal, valley area. Day to day livelihood, eating habits, dressing style and the spirit of home are totally antagonistic. They feel uncomfortable because they can't share their joy and sorrowful moment up to their satisfaction as they can't build up the emotional connection due to the differences in their mindset. There are many parents who are unwilling to fully accept their in-laws as they are. This ideology is characterized in their mood and gesture in their first meeting, then the first impression learned by the in-law is beyond consideration. The future route lies on the first impression, thus the negative observation that the in-law captured in their first meeting provide space to spurt the uncomfortable feelings towards the spouse's parents.

Usually I have difficulty to sleep because of tensions

Tension is a feeling of worry and anxiety which makes people difficult to relax. The origin of tension may be due to distress or uneasiness of mind caused by fear of danger. There are couples who experienced tension,[4] due to nervous and worriment about their decision. They acquainted fear in their life maybe from their real parents or new parents. But now, this tension pushes them into new phase of lives, to live in a sleepless night. Naturally, when a person's psychology is occupied by the fear or tension, even at night the mind can't take proper rest, this rebound back to all the physical, the body and the sight. Consequently, when a person doesn't take a proper rest, it impinges physically and when the body is weak various diseases are contracted leading to possibility of ending their life untimely.

I feel overburdened in life

Every individual has its own capacity. In one's life, the past life experiences helps to go further and it lift them higher. So, to say that, the past life experiences supplement in the present and for the future. Therefore, those who have rich experiences in the past, live better at present. Particularly in the matter of interfaith marriage couple's life, they are overburdened in their new life[5] as their past experiences can't help them in their present because of the differences in culture and tradition. The past life and the new life became totally paradox. Beginning with the natural work till the identity work it became a new world. Thus, it overburdened them. It is just like entering into practical life without theoretical knowledge. Not only in manual activities but psychologically they are overburdened thinking of their own family and spouse's family because such marriages are often not a consented marriage. And when they are psychologically overburdened sometimes it leads to mental impairment.

I am always stressed about my spiritual life

Many of the couples of such marriage feel stressed thinking of their spiritual life.[6] They think that their spiritual life is death as they are married to different religious person so they are so worried. Some female simply converts to their husband's religion without any reasons on faith or desire. Every individual would like to know the status of its spiritual life, but a person who never pray neither worship God will not increase his/her spiritual life rather it will decrease day by day. Sometimes, many Christians wife were forced not to pray, nor to attend church service, such objection disturb their mind to go forward as per their conscience. Because of all these, some couples neither followed the wife's religion nor the husband's religion, and the simply live as atheist. However, although outwardly they live as an atheist, deep inside their heart they are worried about their spiritual life because they don't want their spiritual life to die off.

I am always worried about what is going to happen for my family in the future

Everybody has a plan for future. The labor that rendered today is to make better life in future. Therefore, study was made to enquire whether they are worried about their family life in future. In response to that many of the couples gave clear confirmation that they are worried about what is going to happen for their family in future[7] because they are confused of their belief and the ideology of the spouses and parents may not confirm to the other party. When they are worried too much, tension develops. Exercising over tension in life has less possibility to bring success in life. This (worriment) clearly depicts that there is no 100% commitment among the couples. As per the belief and traditions, some religion accepts divorce and polygamy whereas some religion doesn't. Thus, a person who was brought up in the belief of polygamy have a sense of it and brings insecurity to the spouse. According to Albert Ellis, Rational/Cognitive understanding is the first step that results in either positive or negative emotional feelings. In the case of interfaith marriage, many new spouses feel that they are not completely accepted by the in-laws. So, negative emotions such as feeling guilty and depression develops leading to physical disturbances and improper behavior.[8] Once, when the unexpected behavior is acted out, contrary to the expectation of the family, then it is difficult to work together and bridge the differences. Their discrepancies in thought and action accommodate insecurity and unfaithfulness to live together as one and also in making future plan. If this disparity continues there are high chances of bringing confusion even to the children. In return, the children can be another trouble maker in the future.

I always fear that our children also may end up in interfaith marriage later

Many couples experienced that interfaith marriage has little disadvantages compared to that of the same faith marriage. Often, they had undergone the wrong concept among themselves, and this arranges a way of misunderstanding in all the areas. It's a nature to have conflict within the couples but everything can be sorted out through sacrificial sentiment. Many of this married couples cannot understand each other, they can't differentiate religion, culture, love and family. Indeed, religion is not the only thing that holds two people together, but many people think so and make life complicated. Thus, an enquiry was made for the interfaith marriage couple whether they fear of their children ending up in interfaith marriage, and many couples responded that they are afraid of their children ending up their lives in interfaith marriage.[9] It is because interfaith marriage life is not so successful according to what they have experienced. They do not want their children to end up in this kind of marriage. Hence, they feel scared thinking that the event which they do not want might happen to their children. This fear is a cognitive system and when it develops stronger mental disorder happen eventually.

I am terribly upset with my family life that I think of divorce very often

In fact, none of the couple likes divorce but when the marital life is not going smoothly, without any choice it happens. Outwardly, many people live as a happy married life although it doesn't go well. On this earth, the spouses, families and the nation want married life to be permanent by having good relationship, but when the correlation is not right, unwanted steps are taken and this leaves the family, a broken family. Broken homes have been one of the most serious challenges in today's marriage life. In many of the country, the percentage of broken marriages has been steadily increasing and divorce is also becoming more common. Interfaith marriage is also one of the causes for this. When the spouse is not happy with the in-laws, when the spouses can't live together as blissful, then there is no future, future is ambigious. Then there is no purpose of living together, if it is so, it is better to live a purposeful life by living separately.[10] Therefore, some of the spouse testifies that due to the miserable married life and dejection with the in-law's family, they often think for divorce.[11]

I miss my family members because of my interfaith marriage

One's past cannot be forgotten. Every human has a past history, everyone is a social being with a family who stays together, eat together and spend time together. No matter how many years passes by, the sweet moments that spent together will remain in heart. So, when the family, villager and friends are away for long period of time, everybody miss one another. When people are always around there is not much feeling of missing one another because they see and meet often. But when the people or the dear ones live far away or never see each other frequently, there is a feeling of missing one another. With regard to the spouses of interfaith marriage, many of the spouses reveal that they miss their family members.[12] This clearly proves that because of this marriage many family members don't visit their child. The cause of hesitating in visiting often is due to the differences of culture and faith. The Tribal family members don't feel comfortable to be with the non-tribal lifestyle, similarly the Christians family to the non-Christian family. This statement affirms that there is no proper channel of communication, there is no flow of transparency and there is no demonstration of one family. In short, such marriage has broken the family relationship.

The study on this section shows that there are significant psychological problems because many of the spouses of this marriage reveals that they experienced overburden in their lives due to guilt feeling and the stress makes them worry about their spiritual lives and of family future life. The regret in their marriage leads them to miss their family members and also the tension of their marriage leads them to fear of their children's marriage. They even have the feeling of anxiety and uncomfortable feeling with their partner and with their spouse's parents. There are times where they can't sleep peacefully due to tension in life and of psychological fear. Hence, such married couples' lives are overcome by stress and this psychological fear interrupts their future prospect and due to psychological tension, it makes their natural relaxed behavior impossible.

Social problems

It refers to the problems which affects the couples of interfaith marriages in relation to the society that covers friend circles, leaders from different spheres and the neighboring citizens. Whoever experienced this problem may feel lonely and may yearn for others to visit. Mostly they may feel bored of their lives and assume that they are alone on this earth. Loneliness may even appear as an active power that pursues, overtakes and destroys. Loneliness is a form of sadness. This type of sadness stems from the absence of desired social relationships. The gap in these people's relationship with others will become wider and wider because society usually looks at them negatively and do not need their contribution. On the other side, since they are rejected by the society they also do not want to go forward voluntarily and contribute their views. Some of the social problems are discussed below:

I yearn for somebody to visit and spend time with me

We, being a social and gregarious being everybody need to be with someone. When relatives or friends are around, people hardly feel lonely because whenever they need someone, they always have someone to lean on. But majority of the couples of interfaith marriages feels lonely. This is because people mostly leave them behind and so they really long for somebody to visit them and to spend time with them. As I had mentioned earlier, in such marriages, the family relationship is broken. So even from the old family nobody visits and spend time, identically from the new family too. They yearn for somebody because the both family, friends and even the society left them alone. To be honest, they are just in the middle of the road, neither proceeding nor going back. They received the twin response from both the families, both the family doesn't move forward to be with the couples. There are many people who experiences loneliness only after such marriage. Particularly, the tribal people are communitarian, where they love and prefer to be in a group, visiting and spending time together is one of the unique characteristics, but it was completely opposite for the non-tribal. Therefore, especially those who came from tribal background to the non-tribal, they badly feel lonely and cordially yearn somebody to visit them.[13]

I do not have close friends after marriage

Indeed, friends should be increased after marriage because old friends will remain and as they enter into new generation there is possibility to create new friends circle. However, there are also some cases where people lost their friends after marriage. Particularly, in this marriage many of the spouses lost their close friends and they were left behind with no close friends. Friends weren't happy of such marriage because they didn't encourage such marriages practice. That's the reason why friendship's bond break after the marriage. On the other side, the people of the new family, are unwilling to come forward to bind the rope of friendships as they are from different culture, faith and style of living. This leads them to develop sadness which is a negative emotion and later it turns into mood disorder of depression.[14]

Society have not accepted us totally

The spouses of interfaith marriage reveal that society doesn't accept them totally.[15] Society's acceptance can be seen through delegation of responsibility, cordially welcoming in every social activity. Many spouses considered themselves as innocent, ready to serve and sacrifice for the society but from the perspectives of society, they still have some reservation of doubting the couple to be totally accepted as one of them. There are many incidents where interfaith marriage happened as a plan, particularly to be the informer or to be the trouble makers. Sometimes, it happens to take revenge and to sabotage the entire lineage. The society can't see the whole intuitions of the spouses. Thus, they treat the couple with some kind of reservation and consideration as second-class citizens.

My parents rejected us and are unwilling to share the property due to our interfaith marriage

The rights of handing over the properties or sharing the belonging are in the hands of parents. As per the tribal tradition, the ancestral land or properties can't be given to the woman, but the properties owned by the personal can be given to any children. Most of the parents gives first priority to male child or give more share to the male child, some parents share equally to both male and female child. There are also some parents who share the properties to whom they like or to those who obey them. In the context of interfaith marriage, few couples are not getting any property from the parents as their marriage is not into the likeness of parents.[16] We can clearly understand that such marriage has an objection from the parents, society and friends. When the couple have no one to be supported, then their life is insecure because there will be no one in times of trouble, sorrow and emergency. Their lives are always in danger zone.

There is no one whom I can talk and share about my day to day problems

Serious talk, burning issue and confidential event can be shared only to the close person. It is because they were faithful to one another and were confident that they will receive some relief in return. Also they have trust that they will remain confidential. On this earth, majority of the people have their own faithful friend or person to whom all the grievances can be shared without any suspicion. It is not natural to share the inner problem to the stranger because nothing will be received and it is not wise to reveal all the personal issues to the unknown person because the news can be spread like a wild fire in future. Thus, a statement was collected from the couple of interfaith marriage on whether they have someone to share about their day to day problems and many couples responded that they don't have it.[17] This manifest that they don't have close friends, they don't have a trustworthy person. The society mistreats them and always looks at them with different sight. Hence, their burden always remains in themselves as there is no way to flow off. How painful it will it be, living alone on this vast earth without having a single person to lean on. This is what the present couples of interfaith marriages have been experiencing.

I don't want to participate in any social gathering because they rejected me

As per the current style of living is concerned, people give to those who had given them, love those who loved them, and hate those who hated them. It's a pattern of today's generation to be always parallel in making friends, like doctor and doctor, teacher and teacher, theologian and theologian, poor and poor, rich and rich etc., to be always parallel in harvesting, like hate for hated, love for loved etc. Even in the life of interfaith marriage, there are few couples who don't want to participate in any social gathering simply because the society rejected them. The society doesn't use them so also, they don't want to cooperate.[18] Let's imagine, if this parallel trend remain forever how the society will transform? How the individual life will revive? In fact, individual and society can't be separated, they are two sides of one coin. Individual makes the society and in return society rules and guides the individual.

I don't feel like going out

Certainly, when the relationship with the neighbor and society are not healthy, people dislike going around. Moreover, when someone has no friends circle within the society, he/she is uninterested to go out. There are few couples who testify that they don't feel like going out because of the society's ill-treatment. Sometimes people gossip about the couple, without any reason people laugh at them, people slander about them, tease with derogatory words, turn away from them to refrain from talking, and meeting them is consider as a bad omen. They had done nothing wrong but if they experienced such treatment from society how they will face the people?[19]

I have a low status because of my inter faith marriage

The word status refers to social stratification. Human status can be earned through education, job, occupation, financial status, marital status and fame. Status is related with respect, reverenced and honour. It is understood as the degree of honour or prestige attached to one's position in society. It is a requirement to be with the people, group and organization. There are few societies that ascribe everybody in equal status but most of the societies maintain social stratification in relation to status. They stratified the position as per status, higher position to those who maintain high status, lower position to the weaker.[20] These days there is no value and dignity for the people with low status. Their ideas and knowledge will be discarded, their voices will be unheard. Indeed, to uplift the status is difficult whereas to demolish is very simply. One status can be upgraded through achievement or successful action and at the same time it degrades through one's failure and distractive performances. Many societies consider interfaith marriage as distractive performances so the status of people whoever undergoes such marriages is affected.. Therefore, many couples claim that they are living in a low status because of this interfaith marriage.[21]

There is communication gap between society and us

People's relationship builds through communication. Communication plays an important role in all spheres of human activity. It stands as the root and fruits of all human life realities. It is essential to the development of the individual, to the formation and continued existence of groups and to the inter-relation among groups. The World Council of Churches (WCC) in its 4th assembly at Upssala, stated communication as 'a fabric of life,' this mean that it is by communication we become what we are today. Communication is the lifeblood for our survival in a society, it is like the air we breathe, no communication means no life. Therefore, communication is essential for human living, for human growth, for development and for better relationship. When we communicate with someone, we become one with that person, we become united with that person, we build a community with that person. It is a necessary fundamental for human connection.[22] It is the connection devices that makes oneness person to person, person to society, society to society etc. If there is no communication, it's not possible to understand one another, if they don't understand one another, there is no possibility to build relationship. When there is no relationship people perish. Few couples testify that they don't have proper communication with the society, which shows that there is a barrier between these couples and the society. The causes of this barrier are rejection and ill-treatment. However, one positive thing from the couples' response is although the society doesn't give equal treatment, they are trying to bridge the gap by seeking best sources of communication.[23]

This section also reveals that many of the couples of interfaith marriage experience social problems. Their relationship with the society is not friendly and so they were isolated from the society. As a result, they really yearn for somebody to visit and spend time with them. They lost most of their close friends after marriage and the society do not accept them totally (which means society rejects them partially), and there is no one whom they can talk and share about their day to day problems confidently and also due to this marriage their identity became obscure. Consequently, there are also few couples who experience rejection in sharing the property because of this marriage. Due to the ill-treatment of the society, some couples don't want to participate in any social gathering. As a result, there is a communication gap between society and the couples of interfaith marriages.

Parenting issue

It is about the difficult situation that couple of interfaith marriage comes across in relation to child parenting. The capacity of parents to be adaptable can be affected by wide range of factors like marital conflict, stress, emotional problems and social problems. These factors make parents more vulnerable and decrease parenting capacity. Sometimes they might face rejection of their advice by the children. There is unparallel in understanding as they cannot grasp the idea and reach the ideology of what the children thinks of. Many parents may find it difficult in giving advices to their children due to differences in understanding and due to diverse interest. They may find it difficult in taking full responsibility for the needs of children and subsequently, even the children hesitate to share all their grievances. Thus, the relationship between parents and children may not be in a healthy manner.

My children do not listen to my advice

In present world, many children do not listen to the advice or counsel of their parent, thinking that parent's ideologies or understandings are outdated and not relevant with the present world. They reject parents' advices because they unvalued the worth of the counsel as they don't consider their parents as qualified. Many parents consistently give advice due to their concerns.

On the other side, children gets irritated when parents talk too much untimely. In this generation, there are many children who didn't even talk properly with the parent. They too listen when their parents listen to them, they listen when they develop trust, when they have confidence on their parents. If children listen to their parents' advices it shows that they are respecting parents, they regard parents as an excellent role model. Interfaith married couples testify that their children don't listen to their advices.[24] This proves that, they are disrespected and are considered as unqualified parents by their children. In one sense, it is the influence of the society that makes children devalues their parents. If the children reject parents' words, how will they guide after their children?

I am not able to raise my children well because of our difference in religious identity

Sometimes, differences in religious identity of the couples create difficulties in raising up their children. Religious identity is always related with the self-identity. In one sense, religious identity supplements the person. Every individual's life is molded based on its religious belief. At the same time, the same methods transmit from generation to generation. The method that we were molded shall be using exactly in raising of our children, because that's what we were learned and considered as one of the best. Therefore, if the same faith people marry, together they can easily raise their children as they have and they will know the style of raising. But when two persons from different religious identity come together as couple, mostly, they find it difficult to raise children as they are confused over which method they should apply. This distraction among the couples provides another platform for the children to misuse and cheat the parents. Because of all these predicaments some couples feel alert and reveal that they are not able to raise their children well as per their expectation and aspiration. However, many of the couples adjusted among themselves and find a proper solution for raising children in better way. Thus, although they are from different religious identity, they could raise their children as per their will.[25]

We could not give proper advices to our children due to diverse interest

It is a nature for every individual to have its own unique interest. This interest was instilled from the childhood days in relation to their life experiences, which was shaped by the parents as per their aspiration. Interests are sometimes very much attached with religion because some religious group has restriction for women not to pursue particular profession. Instances, for Hindus, to become a priest it is eligible only from Brahmin Caste, above all no women can be the priest though she is from Brahmin. Whereas, for Christian, they don't have such, everybody can become priest sometimes even women (Rarely), so any gender can pursue theology. Therefore, when the spouses are from different religion as their interest differ, sometimes it also affects in giving advices to the children. Wife's interest may be disliked by husband so also the husband's interest by the wife. If so, good advice for wife can be bad advices for husband. Thus, nothing good comes out and is unable to teach and guide the children accurately. This issue is openly confirmed by some of the couples of interfaith marriages.[26]

Me and my partner disagree many times in punishing our children

Everybody has different method of raising children. As this is the reason, many couples experience disagreement in punishing the children. Some spouse prefers punishing verbally whereas, some prefer through action. These days even in institutions, government warns and circulates rules not to punish the children through action, they are given notice not to used words which can hurt student's sentiment. Such system functions effectively in the cities and urban area. Whereas, in the rural and remote places, people don't care much, there is no proper system, every teacher apply his/her own method of teaching and punishment. At the same time, children of rural areas are naughtier than those of urban. Therefore, many of the teachers use a method of action and sometimes it is more applicable. Such distinction happened even in the family life, if the couples come from different background, rural and urban, they often follow different style of punishing children. In this regard, the author wants to state few techniques of punishing children. Extinction is a punishment style that works well for young children that are seeking to get attention through negative behaviours. Extinction simply means kind ignoring, calling for a parent to withhold their attention from the child until the negative behavior has stopped. Spanking is also another style of punishment performed by the authoritarian parents. Reasoning is another style which is achieved through explaining natural consequences of the behavior of the child. Like, telling children that it will get cold if they don't wear coat. Reasoning makes children realize and understand better.[27] Different people use different style of punishing children. So also, even among the interfaith marriage couple, they apply various ways of punishing children which brings disagreement among them often.[28]

Children are confused of their cultural identity

A study was made from the response of the respondents on the statement "whether children of interfaith marriage are confused of their cultural identity." This statement was asked because the boundaries and jurisdictions of every individual are diverse from one another. Those who are brought in a very conservative atmosphere shall be totally contradicted with those of liberal family. There are some parents who restricted their daughters to wear jeans pant, mini skirt, half-sleeves and t-shirt and trained them to be comfortable with shalwar (long tunic) and saree. Whereas in some family, parents don't much bother on their children's garments. Hindu ladies prefer shalwar (long tunic) and Saree whereas the Christians of North East ladies prefer normal pant and shirt. Muslims are prohibited to eat pork, Hindus are not allowed to slaughter cow (eating is beyond imagination) and Christians are free to eat. As the couples of interfaith belongs to different cultural identity, their lifestyle, dressing, way of talking and eating habits confront one another. When their day to day life of living repudiate then obviously there is a possibility for children to be confused of their cultural identity, as they can't accept neither reject both. This statement has been confirmed by many of the spouses of the interfaith marriage that their children are confused of their cultural identity due to cultural differences of the parents.[29]

Children hardly share their prevalent issues

In this present day, youngsters face different kinds of issues which the older people are ignorant of. Therefore, due to confusion some children share all the prevalent issues to their parents. However, most of the children do not share it and try to tackle it by their knowledge alone. Sometimes the reason of not sharing is due to the distance with the parents, as there are many issues that are considered as taboo. Majority of the children of interfaith marriage hardly share their prevalent issues to their parents, thinking that parents will not be able to give the right solution. So, to say that, children do not have much hope on parents when it comes to present prevalent issues and they keep it in privacy. The world is developing so fast, sometimes ordinary human can't chase after it. In regard to current issues, youngster know much better than the adult parents, the technologies of the present developing world is much closer and familiar to the youngster rather than the adults. The current trends are not so known to the adult, whereas the youngsters are crazy for it. The developing gap and generation gap between children and parents are very much that they make children unwilling to share their prevalent issues. They think that their discerning power and conscience is much sharper and wider than that of parents. There are times when children withdraw their faith from parents thinking that they will not receive answer as per they expect.[30]

There are couples who find difficulty in raising their children as their children don't listen attentively to their advice and disobey their instructions. Due to their diverse interest, they were unable to give good advices to their children. Their psychological problems hinders in the process of parenting. In other words, psychological issues of the couples of interfaith marriages affect the relationship between parents and children. Parenting is related to society because parents and children are convinced by the lifestyles of society. Normally society governs citizens' life, which means that society moulds and influence people. Therefore, if the society is well organized citizens are also well stabled in terms of behavior, mannerism and lifestyles.

Conclusion

This chapter mainly dealt with the scenario and predicament of the couples of interfaith marriages. As per their experiences, it proves that majority of the couples of interfaith marriages faced psychological problems like stress, fear, anxiety, tension and nightmares. Their lives are overcome by stress, psychological fear and interrupt in many of their future prospect. Due to psychological tension it makes their natural relaxed behavior impossible. Also, majority of the couples of interfaith marriages experienced social problems like isolation, loneliness because they were rejected by the society and there is no trustworthy person whom they can confidently trust on. They faced some problem even in parenting as they have unhealthy relationship with their children and the children are unfaithful to understand and listen to their commands. They find it difficult when it comes to parenting issues due to diverse culture and religious background. The differences of parents in culture and religious identity makes the children confuse of their culture and religious identity. This reason let the children withdraw back their hope on parents to ask for the counsel or advice. Thus, the writer concludes that the pastoral care and counseling is essential to aid them, comfort and correct them by teaching, guiding, healing, nurturing, sustaining and empowering them to realize and acknowledge the problems and to confront the problem wisely. Through this means they can live a better life with their family, parents, children, neighbor and society at large.

Endnotes

[1] Appendix, no.1.

[2] Murry, *An Introduction to Pastoral care and Counseling*, 192.

[3] Appendix, no.2.

[4] Appendix, no.3.

[5] Appendix, no.4.

[6] Appendix, no.5.

[7] Appendix, no.6.

[8] D. John Antony, *Psychotherapies in Counseling: Includes Theories of Personality* (Tamil Nadu: Anugraha Publications, 2003), 117.

[9] Appendix, no.7.

[10] J. Russell Chandran, *Christian Ethics* (New Delhi: ISPCK, 2011), 108.

[11] Appendix, no.8.

[12] Appendix, no.9.

[13] Appendix, no.10.

[14] Appendix, no.11.

[15] Appendix, no.12.

[16] Appendix, no.13.

[17] Appendix, no.14.

[18] Appendix, no.15.

[19] Appendix, no.16.

[20] "Social Status," http://www.beyondintractability.org (accessed 01/10/2018).

[21] Appendix, no.17.

[22] L. Imsutoshi Jamir, ed., *A Basic Guide to Communication Studies* (Dimapur: TDCC, 2010), 1.

[23] Appendix, no.18.

[24] Appendix, no.19.

[25] Appendix, no.20.

[26] Appendix, no.21.

[27] Beth Asaff, "Punishment Styles in Parenting," http://www.kids.lovetoknow.com (accessed on 01.11.2018).

[28] Appendix, no.22.

[29] Appendix, no.23.

[30] Appendix, no.24.

CHAPTER - 4

Pastoral Care and Counseling Response

According to the previous chapter, we have seen that the couples of interfaith marriages experienced the psychological, social problems and parenting difficulties. Thus, in this juncture, giving responses from the pastoral care and counseling is essential. The response from pastoral care and counseling would be from the perspective of encouragement to live a better life, supportive for their good life experiences, advices to take good care, to tackle or handle wisely and to provide a means of precaution before they face such unfavorable experiences, with an intention to avoid any unwanted situation. Thus, this chapter deals with response from Pastoral care and Counselling perspective.

Pastoral care response

Pastoral Care is a ministry of mutual healing and growth within and outside of a congregation and its community, through the life cycle. People need pastoral care throughout their lives. It is a response to the need that everyone has for warmth, nurture, support and caring. This need is heightened during times of personal stress and social chaos.[1] It refers to all that a pastor does, including organizing, shepherding the people and communicating the gospel to them. It revolves around the four traditional functions of the Church (Teaching, Proclaiming, Fellowship and Service).[2] It may also be understood as a response to humanity's hurt and search for wholeness. It is an aspect of the ministry of the church which is concerned with the well-being of individuals and of communities in and outside of the church.[3] Thus, pastoral care is for the wholistic ministry irrespective of diverse culture and faith.

Pastoral healing ministry

One of the objectives of Pastoral ministry is to restore the broken relationship, the impair feeling and attitude, heal the emotion and mental impairment, to transform the spiritual aliveness and restore the hatred living atmosphere to wholeness and a peaceful living community. This ministry is not only to heal the physical sickness but healing those who are psychologically disturbed, spiritually departed and has bitter interpersonal relationship. Indeed, pastor is not the healer but is the one who takes the major responsibility for creating the conditions by which healing may occur in the special relationship between the couples and with the in-laws. To bring healing in this tragic situation pastor needs to visit and minister to both the parties, to build up the relationship. When they have mutual relationship, it develops trust and they can depend on one another, they can release the destructive negative emotions, change the hurtful attitudes and develop the sense of living harmoniously.[4] The pastor needs the power of the Holy Spirit in the healing of any sicknesses and crisis. Charles Jefferson said as cited by T.K. Koshy Vaidyan, "the diseases of the soul are numerous, and the remedies provided by the Almighty are efficacious only when applied by a skilled practitioner."[5]

Pastoral sustaining ministry

It is a ministry of helping those who are hurt and it helps in transcending a circumstance in which restoration to his/her former condition or recuperation from his/her malady is either impossible or so remote as to seem improbable.[6] A Pastor is a caretaker or protector not only of his or her own church but even outside his church to live in peace and be fruitful. To let the people, live in peace and live a healthy life, the pastor need to evaluate the past life of the family and find out the root cause of the issue. To sustain their lives healthily, the pastor needs to give guidelines in relation to eating habits, to maintain purity in body and in soul. Pastoral duties also require comforting and encouraging those who are weak, lonely, sorrowful, sick and defeated. No one can take the place of a pastor as he/she brings eternal hope to these people.[7] The sustaining ministry towards the couples of interfaith marriages are called not for consoling nor for curing alone but to live, walk together and thus enriching one another as does each fulfill life's task. This ministry is not necessarily to resolve the situation, but to help them exert their gifts and talents for the society. The role of the care giver is not to concentrate on their problems alone but to look at how they can participate in the society by acknowledging the varied gifts, unique talents and diverse culture.[8]

Pastoral guiding ministry

Particularly, the spouse who comes into the family from other atmosphere, frequently have the sense of inferiority, lower self-esteem and fear. In such context, pastoral guiding ministry is very essential. Advising the original spouse (mostly, groom and his family) and family to be more open and to have the sense of responsibility towards the newly spouse is important. It is also essential to guide the new spouse to be stronger in their determination, to increase communication to all levels, to increase self-esteem, to be wise enough in dealing the situation and to handle the possible problems constructively. Pastoral guiding ministry has to reach both the parties, to develop the sense of mutual trust and belongingness because unless they develop a sense of trust and belongingness, it is hard to bring mutual relationship.[9] The educative guiding seeks to dig the capability and interest of the person rather than using coercion. They do not want to be sympathized or pitied upon but they rather want to be assisted in their own life work by identifying their given interest and talents.[10]

Pastoral reconciling ministry

Pastoral reconciling ministry means helping alienated persons to establish or renew proper and fruitful relationship with God, neighbor and family members. It plays an important part in a person's life as it helps to build bridges between the disputing groups and a solace to the inner conflict inside a person.[11] This kind of ministry needs the concepts of confession and forgiveness. The concept of confession (repentance) and forgiveness in the context of crisis are the ways to resolve the issue. The victims (can be anyone either wife, husband or in-laws) need to develop the sense of forgiveness to the culprit for the mistake done to them. On the other side, the culprits also need to seek forgiveness from the victims, for the mistake they have done to other, to bring reconciliation. Unless there is a sense of genuine forgiveness there is less way of genuine reconciliation and unless there is genuine reconciliation there is less possibility to bring peace. Indeed, the Christian forgiveness needs to be unconditional irrespective of one's confession and repentance. The reconciling work towards these couples includes helping them to reconcile themselves with their consequences because reality simply cannot deny.[12]

Pastoral nurturing ministry

The aim of nurturing is to enable people to develop their potentialities, throughout the life journey with all its joyful and delighted moments and also miserable and sorrowful moments.[13] It can also be defined as the provision of nourishment to a living organism in order to help it to develop and flourish. Pastoral nurturing refers to the task based on the development of the entire sphere (biological, psychological, sociological and spirituality). Nurturing people in order to cope up with the development and changes of physical growth, psychological divergence, different sociological context and of its spiritual life. Sometimes, couples of interfaith marriages are in confused mode due to changes in their psychological thinking, social environment. So, they neither go forward nor draw back but live as it is with no improvement. In this juncture, pastoral provision of nourishment towards those couple is essential in order to grow and to flourish. They cannot be denied or be away from the reality of human's suffering and joy. Pastors need to nurture by educating them on how to confront the reality and face them. Suffering and joy is a part of human's lives. Unless anybody go through those problems, there will not be much development and improvement. Pastors need to feed them with valuable advices to help them tackle their current issues, as well as to be well aware of the possible upcoming issues.[14] The Pastor need to help those couples to adopt a life affirming attitude because even in the midst of helplessness and loneliness there is life as God's grace works for everyone. Nurturing to those people will include teaching about the purpose of their living being in those situations, to let people learn about the wholeness of life through them. Therefore, nurturing them to strengthen their confidence and to have hope of their present life is an urgent task for pastoral work.[15]

Pastoral empowerment ministry

Couples of interfaith marriages are confused about their own life, behavior and future. At this juncture, pastoral empowerment ministry is required to motivate them in deciding what to do and where to go about. Empowerment is a word referring to the energy or force which results in specific behavior, encouraging and inspiring to march forward for the better world. Whatever the situations might be, everybody has physical needs or requirements for the survival. Since, human beings are the social being, everybody needs love from each other and everybody has its own purpose of living no matter what the of different circumstances and situations. Therefore, empowering the couples to put on the zeal of enthusiasm to march forward in order to reach their goal besides their present problems is a necessary task of pastoral care. Self-actualization is one of the main propositions of empowerment which is also one of the highest qualities of humanness to live with full creativeness.[16]

Pastoral counseling response

Pastoral Counseling is one dimension of pastoral care, it is the utilization of a variety of healing (therapeutic) methods to help people handle their problems and crisis and thus experience healing. Pastoral counseling is a preparative function needed when the growth of person is seriously jeopardized or blocked by crisis.[17] It is a specific task within the coverage of Pastoral care. It arises from a crisis situation of the people. It is a caring ministry centered on an individual or group focused on a specific problem. It is a pastoral ministry extended to a person in and outside of the church who need and seek special help.[18] Thus, Pastoral counselor needs to go out in search of those who are in crisis and dilemma not necessarily within the four walls of the church but even outside of the walls. Pastoral counseling can happen anytime, and anywhere so pastoral counselor does not need to wait for the client to visit. They should rather go out and visit those who are in need.

Counseling as a solution to human problems

Counseling aims at helping the clients to understand and accept themselves as they are, such that they are able to work towards realizing their potential. Often this requires modification of attitudes, outlook and behavior. The counselor accepts its clients and has unconditional regard for their personality or self or self-work. Naturally, counseling involves the feelings of clients. It is often because the feelings run so strong that the counseling function becomes a highly delicate and specialized function. In addition to the concern for the feelings of the clients, counseling has a cognitive dimension through which a behavioural change is sought to be achieved. The clients are received without any reservations and they (couples) are helped to state their problems and explore the possible solutions. The counselor does not try to solve the client's problems or make choices that could reduce their emotional conflicts. Instead, through counseling, the clients are helped to discover themselves, their strengths and weaknesses. The self-understanding that is sought to be reached is often through the use of objective psychological instruments. It is generally recognized that an individual has the ability to resolve one's own problems. The counselor aims at making the clients act independently in a mature and responsible manner and with full understanding of the consequences. Counseling aims at helping individuals reach a stage or a state of self-autonomy through self-understanding, self-direction and self-motivation. Thus, client can become a fully functioning person.[19]

Marriage crisis counseling

Marriage is a lifelong union, which involves mutual commitment and trust for each other. But in the present research context, half of the couples undergo different kind of issues, this in return affect the society and family relationship as a whole. This is because many people enter into marriage with certain misconceptions, lack of maturity and knowledge, which can damage their relationship and create an atmosphere of disillusionment and unhappiness. Marriage counseling must look to the inter-personal relationships for developmental and integrative life in the intimacy of association such as love and affection, sexual relations, emotional inter dependence and temperamental interaction. Marriage counseling is a form of guided interaction between the spouses to see that the individual meets the roles in marriage and to adjust adequately the individual to the roles. It is a process in which a counselor helps couples and families to make plans and solve problems inside the marriage relationship.[20] The counselor's goal includes, identifying and understanding the specific issue which are creating problems; teaching the couple how to communicate constructively; teaching problem-solving and decision making techniques; helping the couples to express their frustrations, disappointments and desires for the future. When the counselor clears with the goal, it is easier to concentrate on counselee's goal. When both the spouse set their goal in-line with the counselor, it is easier to attain the goal because the couple can learn about constructive communication and problem solving in the process.

Here is the proposed process of marriage crisis counseling

STAGE I: The beginning

The counselor seeks to establish rapport through warm, accepting, trusting, uncritical, understanding attitude and to help the counselees overcome initial fears.

The counselee must share his/her initial reasons for seeking help and must overcome initial fears and doubts related to seeking help.

STAGE II: Emergence of basic problems

The counselor encourages detailed discussions of specific conflict situations and expressions of feelings, raises questions or makes comments to stimulate further thought and to clarify both issues and feelings, continues to give support and encouragement.

The counselee gives more details, expresses feelings and frustrations, learns to build a trusting, secure relationship with the counselor.

STAGE III: Developing and trying tentative solution

The counselor continues to be supportive and alert to new information but encourages and guides in the consideration of tentative solutions such as attitude change, behavior change, confession, forgiveness, reexamination of perceptions etc. guides and encourages as solutions are attempted, evaluated and tried again (both in the counseling sessions and at home).

The counselee learns how to formulate, act on and evaluate solutions, expresses frustrations and fears as they arise, experiences some victories.

STAGE IV: Termination

The counselor encourages the counselees to launch out without the counselor, reviews past progress, expresses the counselor's continued availability if needed.

The counselee expresses doubts and fears in going out from counseling but reevaluates progress and examines one's spiritual and personal resources for getting along without counseling.[21]

Supportive counseling

In Supportive care and counseling, the pastor uses methods that stabilize, undergird, nurture, motivate, or guide troubled persons-enabling them to handle their problems and relationships more constructively within whatever limits are imposed by their personality resources and circumstances. Supportive Counseling helps people to gain the strength and perspective to use their own psychological and interpersonal resources more effectively in coping creatively with their life situations. In supportive counseling the pastor makes more use of guidance, information, reassurance, inspiration, planning, asking and answering the questions, and encouraging or discouraging certain forms of behavior.[22] The purpose of this counseling is to support the individual, socially, emotionally and spiritually. In this counseling, good listening skill is very much needed for both the feelings and of the verbal. In this counseling, people find strength, motivation, stability and direction in difficult times.[23] Pastor need to support the couples of interfaith marriages through nurturing, motivation and guiding to enable them to handle their problems and relationship more constructively. Supporting does not mean to go ahead with this kind of marriage, neither to collaborate with their stand and ideology. Instead, it gives correction, encourage to be more flexible in their decision and lifestyles. Thus, this counseling support for the better life union, to have vast future aspects by maintaining good relationship with spouse, family and also with the society. The goal of this counseling is to help persons gain the strength and perspective to use their psychological and interpersonal resources more effectively in coping creatively with their life situation.[24] In Supportive Counseling the counselor help the couple to accept his or her partner with his or her limitation, also to accept in-laws by seeing their limitations, in order to adjust to certain situation in the marriage which cannot be changed.[25]

Crisis counseling

The crises that the couples of interfaith marriages are going through (may not be all the couples) are both developmental and situational crisis. Therefore, the response here will be given in general, particularly from the perspective of intervention. Crisis in human lifetime is a must but humans should try to take it in positive ways by any means. In a sense that, crisis should be taken as a challenge in equipping for the better life. Conversely, majority of the people take it in negative , thereby leading to discouragement, frustration and depression. There is a creator God (for every religion) whom all the human being relies and takes refuge. Every individual will experience crisis in different ways, but creator God will guide everyone in times of troubles and crisis by granting wisdom and discerning power to handle and cope with the situation wisely. God knows where humans are, and he also knows the exact nature of its consequences. God always cares and thus, he will never leave anyone. As for humans, when they cannot handle certain situations they interpret it as crisis. Indeed, it is not, it's so called developmental arrangement, and this will not happen all the time and will not last forever, rather it will be for some time. As the couples of interfaith marriages enter to new environment, they usually faced difficulty in adjusting ideology and in building relationship, but this is not a crisis instead it is a process of development for humanity's growth. Difficult circumstances have the ability to produce perseverance, character and hope. In fact, this hope helps people to look ahead, to face the crises that are so much a part of life in this world.[26]

Behavioural couples counseling

To response from this kind of approaches, counselor assess the strength and weaknesses of the couple's relationship. Couples can be coached to give positive feedbacks. Dysfunction of the couple's relation and also with in-laws is the result of low rates of positive reinforcement. A major treatment strategy is to increase positive control while decreasing the rate of aversive control. Another major strategy is to improve communication, which is hoped to facilitate the couples' ability to solve problems. To intervene from the trouble, couples need to be taught to express themselves in clear behavior descriptions, rather than in vague and critical complaints. They need to be taught to adopt new behavior exchange procedures emphasizing positive, in place of aversive, control. They need to be encouraged to establish clear and effective means of sharing power and making decisions and they need to know new strategies for solving future problems, as a means of maintaining and extending gains initiated in therapy. Their disagreement and angry exchanges may not be harmful in the long run, because dissatisfaction at the present may be getting well later. However, defensiveness, stubbornness and withdrawal from conflict lead to long-term deterioration in marriages. Therefore, couples need to be specific, express requests in positive terms, respond directly to criticism instead of cross-complain, talk about the present and the future rather than the past, listen without interruption, minimize punitive statements and eliminate questions that sound like declarations.[27]

Logo therapy

Logo therapy was developed by a Jewish psychotherapist, Victor E. Frankl. It is a psychological, therapeutic treatment comprising a spiritual approach to the root of the problem, which help people appreciate their responsibility for existence, gain liberty out of emotional distress, and find meaning and purpose of their life. Logo therapy aims at healing a person by helping them finding meaning, the purpose of their life, and making them commit to their realization.[28] Frankl promulgate that life has meaning under all circumstances and the central motivation for the living is the 'will to meaning', the freedom to find meaning in all that we think and the integration of body, mind, and spirit. It aimed at challenging individuals to find meaning and purpose through, among other things, suffering, work and love.[29] The main objective of logo therapy was to facilitate client's quest for meaning and empower them to live meaningfully, responsibly, regardless of their life situations.[30] Therefore, logo therapy can be helpful for those coupls who are facing different kinds of issues, particularly couples of interfaith marriage who faces psychological and sociological problems, in order to find their real identity and meaning of their life.

Rational emotive behaviour therapy: irrational to rational belief

Albert Ellis is an American Psychology, who proposed the Rational Emotive Therapy Behaviour theory. He proposed this theory in such a way that people need to reveal and break down the irrational beliefs that lead to distress. This theory proves that the irrational belief of the people causes real suffering. Albert Ellis states that, it is not the event that affects a person rather it is how the person thinks about the events. Therefore, the main humanity's problems lie in how people develop and accept its thinking power towards others, new life and new environments.[31] He concentrated on individual's perceptions and interpretations of events that occur in the family. In this method, family members are treated as individuals, each of whom prescribes to a particular set of beliefs and expectations. The family members realize that their illogical beliefs and distortions serve as the foundation for their emotional distress. This method illustrates that it is not the events that cause emotional distress but the beliefs about the events. Therefore, they are assisted to dispute their irrational beliefs. By this method they are put on a more rational basis. The counselor teaches the family actively and directly those emotional problems caused by irrational beliefs. By changing these self-defeating ideas, they can improve the overall quality of the family relationship.[32]

For the couples of interfaith marriages, the problems arise due to the irrational thinking and beliefs develop by each of the spouse or by the in-laws. When they develop and accept irrational thought towards one another, for sure the outcome will be a problematic and undesirable impact. When the couples develop the sense of differences from other people and of the friends, then the responses from others will always be negative, and it may create problem. Therefore, to settle down the issue or in order not to have the issue, to have a better relationship and to live a healthy life, everyone needs to change the irrational thinking to rational thinking. Minimizing the concepts of self-defense outlook, they must proceed on to acquire a more realistic thought. This can be done by letting the persons to rethink repeatedly, the things that they have done and the thought that they are thinking, of being themselves as well as of being others. To change the irrational to rational belief, everyone needs to adopt the sense of empathy. To recognize the significance or the pain of other person not only from outward sense but experiencing and understanding through inward. The rational thought can protect one's life because it keeps away from the thought that is going to hurt other. Rational Emotive Behavior Therapy focuses on the present and says that, mostly those irrational thinking transmitted from the past and bring conflict in present. Therefore, Rational Emotive Behavior Therapy focuses and suggests enjoying one's life to live together peacefully and survive one's life by having mutual relationship with one another.[33]

Transactional analysis: life position

Transactional Analysis was founded by Eric Berne, an American Psychiatrist and Psychoanalyst as well. He propounded four life positions, "I'm not ok, you're ok", "I'm not ok, you're not ok," "I'm ok, you're not ok" and "I'm ok, you're ok". In the present research context, half of the new wedded wives of the interfaith marriage perceives the position of "I'm not ok, you're ok", which means they see others as well adjusted and effective but sees themselves as maladjusted and ineffective. These people feel helpless and powerless in comparison to others and they withdraw from confrontations rather than competing. So, they normally become depressed and they themselves live in isolation from others. Whereas on the other side, half of the husband or the in-laws have the position of "I'm ok, you're not ok", which means considered themselves as effective but see others as ineffective. They give little or no respect for the wives and so they easily and frequently find fault with the wives. They are supportive of themselves but hardly do they accept support from the new wives. Thus, there are miscommunication, and this make issues in most of the time. Nevertheless, to live healthy and peaceful life, they both need to change from this kind of life position to normal and healthy position, "I'm ok, you're ok" (the winner position). It is because this life position approach and solve problems constructively. They have valid expectation about themselves and other and accept themselves and others as good, worthy and significant human being. They enter freely into meaningful relationship with others because they find neither inferior nor superior to others rather, they feel worthy of themselves and of others as well.[34]

Solution focused therapy

This counseling was propounded by Insoo Kim Berg, a Korean psychologist and Steve De Shazer, a Milwaukee psychologist.

Majority of the counselors are trained to focus on problem solving and so they see client as the problems. However, counsellor involved in solution focused therapy focuses on solution, which means it focuses on clients' strength and help clients identify their preferred goals, and help them recognize that their lives have not been filled only with problems, rather there have been times when they have been strong, felt good about themselves and have dealt effectively with issues that have been arisen. Thus, counselor of this counseling is to inquire about those times and to help clients see how they have effectively coped so that such mechanisms can potentially be amplified and used in the future.[35] This counselor assists clients to shift from 'problem talk' (trying to understand or analyze their problems) to 'solution talk' (focusing on what is working or could work in the future) as quickly as possible. The fact is that, when one focuses its attention on solution, it eliminates problems. Counselor will not provide imposing solution but have trust on client that by sharing the elements of problems they will find their own way. Counselor tries to turn the elements of problems to the elements of solution.[36] Human lives are filled with changes (physical, psychological, environment), so it is a must to undergo issues (unexpected issues develop from situational changes) as we move through. However, human needs to changes its attitude towards the issues and consider it as a mechanism for human's betterment or recognize it as opportunity. Thus, the couples can try out new behaviours and new ways as they direct their lives to the directions they want to take themselves.[37]

Problem solving approach

This counseling approach was propounded by Singaporean counselor, Anthony Yeo. This counseling has a unique strategy and direction. It focuses on a particular problem, besides other several problems. Thus, the process is more concrete, tangible and more manageable. To give counseling to the couples of interfaith marriages from this approach, counselor has to prepare to try anything to bring changes in the life of counselee. Normally in other approach, counselee leads by talking about his or her problems while the counselor responds empathetically and draw counselee to keep talking. But in this approach, the client needs direction from the counselor so that the counselee can disclose appropriate information for the purpose of problem-solving. This approach requires proper appointment, structure for the session with an intention that the counselee will generate solution by providing recommendation and strategies to help the counselee.

This approach focuses on the reframing of the situation, which means focuses on the change of counselee's conceptual and emotional context in which the situation is experienced. Sometimes, due to negative attitude towards the spouse and in-laws, problem can be created anytime out of nowhere and it makes the problem more severe because negative thoughts invite negative conception and understanding. When the counselor could change this from negative to positive view it can reduce the intensity of the problem. Couples of interfaith marriages tend to feel that they are overwhelmed by the problems and so become immobilized. In this juncture, reframing of their attitude towards the problem defuses the intensity and gives the counselee a sense of control over it. It provides them the new hope to cultivate the courage of overwhelming the problem.

The most important focal point of a counselor is to help the couples to change the view of the problem not as destructive drive but as a developmental device. When the counselee changes the concept towards the problem, positive view develops. The entire issues will no longer be considered as destructive factor rather it will be considered as constructive factor. Thus, it will make the response productive as they view from positive aspects and help them to lighten the value of the problem. This motivates the counselee to normalize the situation and encourage moving one step closer to the recovery zone. Normally, people tend to be too severe when they have problem although the problem itself is not that serious. Those who are depressed and stressed usually feel abnormal and their daily schedule is easily disturbed leading to more disorganization for their life.

Once the counselor has assessed the problem with the counselee, counselor should engage the counselee in talking about the cost of change. Counselee should ask to think the negative consequences that will accrue in his/her life situation. The counselee should be allowed to rethink of their normal daily activities, plan out the daily activities which he/she prefers to live like and persuade him/her to make the comparison between the present daily activities and the propose of daily activities. After the evaluation encouragement should be given to the counselee to live as per his/her desire with an objective to evaluate the changes in daily life. They should be provided the hope of change by revealing the counselee's strength with an affirmation that every situation is not out of control because everybody has a power and strength to deal it. Thus, with this sense of courage and revelation, counselee will realize its potential and capability to handle and empower the problem.[38]

Counseling the depressed person

Depression appears to grip the will and the ability to think. Consequently, it affects not only feelings but also behavior. People exhibit many varying symptoms. They may sleep less or irregularly, lose concentration, find no pleasure in personal relationship or their normal treat, do not feel like eating and feel a sense of worthlessness. And their depression is triggered due to the bitter or broken relationship with the spouse and family. Mostly, depressed persons are not capable of taking steps against the source of depression.[39] Depressed people need help, their erratic behavior notwithstanding, they require the support of those around them, even though their actions make it difficult. Some will display an angry or irritable face that rebuffs their friends when they need them most. One's assistance is more valuable at that point than at any other time.[40]

To counsel those people, counselor need to provide friendship, warmth and help to formulate new plan for living. Counselor can help them to look at the situation or the incident (where they develop depression) differently from another angle or direction. If the spouse of interfaith marriage develops depression due to angriness towards the spouse or in-laws, the best way of remedy to this case is to forgive the culprit.[41] The most important things counselor can do for a depressed person is to be present when he/she needs it. No matter how much he/she reacts adversely to your presence, he/she needs you to save him/her from his/her self-destructive emotions, mental attitudes and physical violence. Counselor need not talk or probe or offer advice to be of help, but its presence during a time of intense despondency affords mute evidence of counselor's love and will tend to counteract the rejection that has contributed to his depression.[42] Counselor's comforting can help fight depression. Thomas House, a senior lecturer in applied Mathematics at the University of Manchester says, as cited by Julie Beck, someone's accompaniment can protect from depression and this give them courage to take new steps to recover from depression. The comforting words like, "I will be there for you during your difficult situation, intolerable moments and unexpected circumstances."[43] The counselor should not sympathize with him/her or help them justify their self-pity but at the same time they should not be condemned. They require understanding and empathy and not condemnation. Be encouraged but do not argue, be gentle and understanding.[44] Thus, providing a sense of protection by accompanying with them, being available in almost all their needs and giving lots of comforting words will helps the depressed people to recover from it.

Counselors must be self-aware in order to provide effective services. Paradoxical intention is also often used by the marriage crisis counselors. It helps to change the "meaning of situation and open up new behavioural alternatives." If a counselor gives permission to a couple to argue, they will freely exchange all their negative feeling and unhappy incidents. This alleviates feelings of anxiety and guilt. Ironically, the negative feelings may subsequently subside and fighting may decrease. Reframing of problems helps couples gain new perspectives and better problem-solving abilities. Counselors must bear in mind that when using reframing, they must present the context in a manner and format accepted by clients. One simple example of reframing using a mere word to alter one's subjective experience is to help a client define a struggle as a 'challenge' or 'opportunity for growth' rather than a 'problem.' Counselors need to help couples identify current issues and assist them in focusing on the here and now. Couples need to learn about issues and behaviors that undermine a marriage. Counselors need to be in a position to educate, promote positive change and provide couples with the opportunity to evaluate their relationships and make positive changes, regardless of their differences.[45]

The goal of counseling to the couples of interfaith marriage is to help the couple involve in working out solution to their problems (self, interpersonal, psychological and social problem) to the advantage of each one, both interpersonally and legally.[46] It also help couples learn how to make their relationship more mutually satisfying in relation to family members and society to bring healing (all their problems) by redefining their view perspectives towards the issues, to experience fulfillment and satisfaction. It is not only to solve the present problems but also to tackle the problem wisely by providing skills.[47] It is to build up the emotional bond to have proper communication among the couples, with the society to restrain from bitter feelings, to response together the challenges that they faced, to consider the issues as a gifts for development, to develop the sense of equality through rational thinking by seeking the meaning of life regardless of its circumstances and consequences. It is to free the individual from unconscious restrictions so that everyone will be able to interact with one another as whole, healthy persons on the basis of current realities rather than unconscious images of the past.

Majority of the couples of interfaith marriage experienced psychological, sociological problems and parenting difficulties. In return it affects in their ongoing life relationship, because sometimes due to psychological affects all the discussion does not go smoothly, directing it to negative aspects. And later this develops in their hearts and widens their relationship. It develops anxiety disorder, phobic disorders, obsessive compulsive disorder, guilt feeling and major depression, inferiority complex and fear of future. On the one side, couples are experiencing the cross-cultural problems because society is not willing to accept them as one fully active mate due to their diverse interest and culture. In return, it affects in their societal relationship and makes them lonely. Society does not feel free to talk about the confidential issues along with them because society does not have trust on them. On the one side, even the couples do not have a trustworthy person to share all the privacy and confidential problems. Thus, these kinds of treatment make them a second-class citizen. Some couples even find difficulty in raising their children as their children don't listen attentively to their advice and disobey their instructions. Because of their diverse interest, they are unable to give good advices to their children and are unable to take a core responsibility to the needs of their children, find difficulty in giving disciplinary control and in taking disciplinary actions. As they have diverse ways of raising children, they couldn't understand their children fully and couldn't maintain good relationship with them.

Thus, seeing all these serious issues, the church leaders and pastors should not remain silent and not simply act as silent spectator. Rather they need to extend its care and counseling, rejecting the traditional view of pastoral care and counseling, which was normally performed confining within the Church membership jurisdiction. Indeed, by the ministry of pastoral care and counseling, they will enhance new knowledge and power, receive the courage to face different issues and develop the ability to consider the problems as a sign of development which is a must in human's lifetime. It will also develop positive outlook, to see all the issues as a gift from above to develop wisdom, reasoning power and to bridge the gap deeper and stronger.

Endnotes

[1] Howard Clinebell, *Basic types of Pastoral Care and Counseling* (Nashville: Abingdon Press, 1984), 27, 48.

[2] Murry, *An Introduction to Pastoral care and Counseling*, 164.

[3] Sumi, "A study on the Psychological problems of widows in Sumi community", 96.

[4] L.K. Graham, "Healing," in *Dictionary of Pastoral care and counseling*, edited by Rodney J. Hunter (Bangalore: Theological Publications of India, 2007), 500.

[5] T.K. Koshy Vaidyan, *A Pastoral Theology and Manual* (Hyderabad: Authentic books, 2013), 128. (Hereafter, Vaidyan, *A Pastoral Theology and Manual*).

[6] Zubeno Kithan, *Pastoral Care and Counseling* (West Bengal: SCEPTRE, 2013), 32. (Hereafter, Kithan, *Pastoral Care and Counseling*).

[7] Vaidyan, *A pastoral theology and manual,* 129.

[8] Ezamo Murry, "the role of Tribal Pastors towards Persons with disability,"*Journal of Tribal Studies,* vol. xiv, No. 2 (2009), 19. (Hereafter, Murry, "the role of Tribal Pastors towards Persons with disability,").

[9] Clinebell, *Basic types of Pastoral Care and Counseling,* 358.

[10] Ezamo Murry, "The role of Pastors in caring for persons with disability," *Embracing the inclusive community: A disability perspective,* edited by Wati Longchar and R. Christopher Rajkumar (Bangalore: SATHRI, 2010), 110.

[11] William A. Clebsch and Charles R. Jaekle, *Pastoral Care in Historical perspective: An essay with exhibits with a new preface by the authors* (New York: Harper & Rows publishers, 1964), 56.

[12] Kethoser Kevichusa, "Forgiveness in the absence of justice and reconciliation: An ethical exploration with special reference to the issue of Naga Political murders," *Violence and Peace: Creating a culture of Peace in the contemporary context of violence,* edited by Frampton F. Fox (Bangalore: Asian Trading Corporation, 2010), 20.

[13] Kithan, *Pastoral care and counseling,* 32.

[14] R.R. Osmer, "Education, Nurture and Care," *Dictionary of Pastoral Care and Counseling,* edited by Rodney J. Hunter (Bangalore: Theological Publications of India, 2007), 337.

[15] Murry, "the role of Tribal Pastors towards Persons with disability," 22.

[16] Larry Crabb, *Effective Biblical Counseling* (Hyderabad: Authentic Books, 2011), 78-79.

[17] Clinebell, *Basic types of Pastoral Care and Counseling,* 27.

[18] Murry, *An Introduction to Pastoral care and Counseling,* 164.

[19] S. Narayana Rao, *Counseling Psychology* (New Delhi: Tata McGraw Hill Publishing Company Limited,1984), 33.

[20] John, *Spirituality of marriage,* 129.

[21] Gary R. Collins, *Christian Counseling: A comprehensive* guide (Texas: Word Books Publisher, 1980), 179.

[22] Enokali, "A study on the Psychological problems faced by childless couples among Sumi community: Implication for Pastoral Care and Counseling" (M.Th. Thesis, Clark Theological College, Aolijen, Mokokchung, 2015), 86.

[23] R.S. Sullender, "Supportive counseling," Dictionary *of Pastoral Care and Counseling,* edited by Rodney J. Hunter (Bangalore: Theological Publications of India, 2007), 1244.

[24] Clinebell, *Basic types of Pastoral Care and Counseling,* 27.

[25] Charles William Steward, *The Minister as Marriage Counselor: A role-relationship theory of marital Counseling and Pastoral Care* (Nashville: Abingdon press, 1983), 82-83.

[26] Scott Floyd, *Crisis Counseling: A Guide for Pastors and Professionals* (Grand Rapids: Kregel Publications, 2008), 39.

[27] John Antony, *Family Counseling: the Classic School* (Tamil Nadu: Anugraha Publications, 2005), 92. (Hereafter, Antony, *Family Counseling: the classic school,*)

[28] Anthony Mannarkulam, eds., *Hand Book of Counseling and Psychotherapies* (Kottayam: Sanjivani Rehabilitation Center, 1997), 185.

[29] Gerald Corey, *Theory and Practice of Counseling and Psychotherapy*, 135.

[30] D. John Antony, *Psychotherapies in Counseling: Includes Theories of Personality* (Tamil Nadu: Anugraha Publications, 2003), 220.

[31] Cliffort T. Morgan, *Introduction to Psychology* (New Delhi: Mc Graw Hill Education Pvt. Ltd., 2014), 706.

[32] Antony, *Family Counseling: the Classic School*, 93.

[33] Y.M. Edison, *Pastoral Counselling* (New Delhi: ISPCK, 2011), 47.

[34] Murry, *An Introduction to Pastoral Care and Counseling*, 192.

[35] Edward Neukrug, *Counseling Theory and Practice* (New Delhi: Cengage Learning, 2012.),430. (Hereafter, Neukrug, *Counseling Theory and Practice,*)

[36] Antony, *Family Counseling: the Classic School*, 113.

[37] Neukrug, *Counseling Theory and Practice*, 433.

[38] Anthony Yeo, *Partners in life* (Goa: APECA Publications, 1993), 23. (Hereafter, Yeo, *Partners in life,*)

[39] William K. Kay, Paul C. Weaver, *Pastoral Care and Counseling* (Secunderabad: OM Authentic books, 2007), 168 (Hereafter, Kay, Paul C. Weaver, *Pastoral Care and Counseling*).

[40] Tim Lahaye, *How to win over Depression* (Secunderabad; Authentic Books, 2008), 238. (Hereafter, Lahaye, *How to win over Depression*).

[41] Kay, Paul C. Weaver, *Pastoral Care and Counseling*, 168.

[42] Lahaye, *How to win over Depression,* 239.

[43] Julie Beck, "How friendship fight depression," *The Morung Express,* Nagaland, August 21, 2015.

[44] Lahaye, *How to win over Depression*, 243.

[45] Tammy J. Shaffer, "Interfaith Marriage and Counseling Implications," http:www.citeseerx.ist.psu.edu (accessed on 22/10/ 2014).

[46] Charles William Stewart, *The Minister as marriage counselor* (Nashville: Abingdon Press, 1970), 81.

[47] Everett Worthington, *Christian Marital Counseling* (Secunderabad: OM books, 2002), 189 & 191.

CHAPTER - 5

Proposal for Peaceful Coexistence

We have seen the scenario and the difficulties that the interfaith marriages couples went through. Thus, in relation with the problems the responses has been given from the Pastoral Care and Counseling point of view, from various approaches. In this chapter, the recommendation is made for couples of interfaith marriages, particularly to avoid harm in their life by adopting positive consideration towards the worldly problems and differences. Also, for the Church elders to look with positive outlooks towards those couples by considering their ministries from wholistic aspects, irrespective of active and passive members of the Church. At last, it was given for the unmarried youth to be more alert before taking any further steps to avoid unfavorable circumstances.

Recommendations for the couples of interfaith-marriage

Growing the sense of couple as one body

What are the challenges where the husbands and wives of the interfaith marriage need to work together to grow in the process of oneness? Particularly, their two unique individuals with different temperaments and personalities, upbringing in culture and religious background, past emotional baggage, parents and in-law's interference, conflicts, unrealistic expectations, incompatibility and unforgiveness. When there is no meaningful growth in marriage, it becomes a weak and a cold marriage which fails to have proper contact with society. It widen the relationship and affects the life of the children psychologically and it even affects the legacy for the next generation. Some of the practical suggestions to help keep growing closer to each other could be, continuous sharing of significant happenings of the day, setting aside time for family discussion and prayer, sharing its struggles, difficulties, desire and concerns, surprising each other with gifts on special occasions, doing the household work together, making fun games or entertaining together.[1]Male and female are created differently they both have complementary qualities. So, to say that, their differences never makes one gender complete unless they unit. Sharing and expressing one's need is very important, thus verbal communication and body languages builds the relationship. When there are any lingering issues in relationship that have not been dealt with properly, one should be the first person to say sorry. Physical intercourse is one way of togetherness as one. It has the power to create intense emotional and spiritual bonds. However, careless handling of sex has the power to completely melt down marital relationship.[2]

Learning to live with differences

Ultimately, the key to success in an interfaith parent-child relationship is to learn to live with differences. Learning to be tolerant and understanding of the religious, cultural and spiritual practices of other is always a challenge. It is even a bigger challenge when somebody has an emotional reaction to every religious decision that the child makes because the child's choice may becontrary to his or her own. The key to learning to live with differences is learning emotional flexibility. Sometimes, it is very hard to watch the child saying prayers from another religious tradition, participating in different and unfamiliar religious rituals and customs. However, emotional flexibility and tolerance is absolute crucial, and it can be a lifesaving skill to cultivate. This emotional flexibility can be shown with positive attitude. Due to the child's different ideas, behavior and decision, the parent can be upset and they develop feeling of guilt. Nevertheless, positive attitude creates good relationship with the children, in-laws irrespective of their differences.[3]

Preparation for happy married life

Every marriage has its share of marital conflicts, its ups and down. To be forewarned is to be forearmed. After having prayerfully discussed all the vital issues one can definitely conclude whether the couple contemplating marriage is compatible or not. If the points on which they differ for exceed the ones, on which they agree they must seriously reconsider the plans. Being married does not give a spouse the right to own the other person. Respect the partner's ability to think and act rightly. Nobody likes to feel like a possession. In a relationship where there is love, there should be equality as well. One of the traits of unhappy couples is that one treats the other like a child. in a relationship where one is considered as inferior and the other as superior cannot be in a happy married life. A married life consists of two equal partners mutually loving and respecting each other. The success of a marriage does not depend only on choosing the right partner but also on becoming the right partner. There can be no happy married life without trust. To the one who is trusted comes security from a relationship based on understanding. Trust in one's spouse is transforming, and it reaps far reaching benefits. Trust begets trust and an interesting side effect of trust in an instinctive inability to betray the other's trust, which leads to happy married life.[4]

Coping with the feeling of guilt

One of the most important challenges for the couples of interfaith marriages is the challenge of coping with the feeling of guilt. This is because, when it comes to interfaith marriage and the dynamics between parents and children, everyone seems to find something to feel guilty about. Sometimes, in-laws and children may disobey the decision or the instruction that the couple give. In such case, they develop the feeling of guilt. However, in contrast to the feeling of guilt, they should be given respect and trust. To treat them with respect means to give them the right to make their own decisions and then to live with the consequences of those decisions. Guilt comes when their views are imposed upon others and when it is not done. Therefore, to let the feeling of guilt go away, they should be given the ability to be their own independent human being, freely making their own decision and choices. This does not mean to be totally away from them. Opinion sharing and giving counsel can be done but force system should not be applied.[5]

Consider differences as gifts

Obviously, couples of interfaith marriages will experience differences in terms of habits, thoughts, likeness and beliefs. However, one of the ways in which the couples can help in creating a family's harmony is by understanding differences not as problems but as gifts. They are opportunities and not just barriers or stumbling blocks. Every issue can become an opportunity to reinforce one's love, one's family support and willingness to go the extra mile to serve as a source of comfort, security and stability in the midst of religious negotiations and family stresses. Ultimately, it is the successful manner to confront and resolve its differences. The challenge of interfaith life is to create harmony out of difference, to create mutual respect and love in the midst of ambiguity and paradox. Interfaith life provides an opportunity for the couple to learn and grow, expanding one's understanding of others.[6]

Effective parenting

Parenting is essentially an ongoing battle between the hopes that parents build for the children and the fears that haunt parent's mind about translating those hopes into realities. Ellen Goodman as cited by Devaraj has rightly said, "The central struggle of parenthood is to let our hopes for our children outweigh our fears." When that is rendered impossible on account of parents, parenting becomes unpleasant and burdensome job. Parents should not let them overcome by the fears that haunt their minds in regard to raising their children effectively. They should rather lighten their hearts and minds with the undying flame of hope that they will be able to influence their children positively and bring them up beautifully. Disciplining the children and making them grow into specimens of unparallel beauty is the need of the hour. To lead children into well-disciplined and value-centred lives, parents need good exemplary life. It is because many a time due to worse and wicked environment children were mislead to wrong direction.[7] To many parents, discipline means punishment. But, actually, "to discipline means to teach." Rather than punishment, discipline should be a positive way of helping and guiding children to achieve self-control. Discipline requires parents to recognize the requirements for successful living and then to create or allow experiences that provide guidance. These experiences should include activities within an emotionally bonded relationship and consequences for a child's behavior.[8]

Parenting is a 24-hour intensive and sacrifice-involved care giving exercise that places no conditions and it builds up no expectation. A moment of carelessness, negligence and timidity like when the parents are not capable of raising their children well, could not give good advices and could not take responsibility of the children any longer, parenting could end up in disaster. John Locke, as cited by Deveraj rightly said, "Parents wonder why the streams are bitter, when they themselves have poisoned the fountain." Thus, when children go astray, the main cause is the indifference and negligence of their parents. Many people confidently claim that the crisis in the family is because of parents themselves, because if parents are vigilant and patient, parenting is bound to an unsurpassable sense of accomplishment and fulfillment. Being a parent, they need to have the strength and the sense of responsibility for the children and have the capacity to raise the children, give advice and disciplinary action. They are the core person to maintain good relationship among them.[9]

Maintain good relationship with the in-laws

The parents might have been unhappy of the marriage because of the difference in religion. Due to their disagreement and anger, the outcome might be disapproving, and the treatment might be unconstructive. However, such issue will not be a problem in the long run since it is for temporary. There is a possibility to create close relationship from the spouse, by any means they should not reflect back to their disagreement and anger. Rather they need deep understanding of why they are angry. and take the full responsibility to take care of their lives, despite the depressing, sad and joyous moments. It is good to always consider the in-laws as their own parents and never leave them alone, materially, physically and emotionally. Never hide any agenda from them, be open in all the matters for better transparency. As you join to the family as one, live passionately and toil for the success of the house. Remain content to obey, serve and correct them to build up a better family and to have peace and love in the family.[10]

Resolving conflict

Two people brought up in two different homes differing in many ways are bound to be different and personality clashes at times. It is normal to have conflict in marriage. Being in an interfaith marriage, couples need to go through a number of adjustments, like differences in aptitudes, background, ways of doing things, life experiences and the role models which they inherit from their parents. Therefore, tensions, argument, feeling of anger, hurt and frustrations are inevitable and sometimes they are quite painful. But these are sign of the fact that they care for each other. What they need to do is to understand those differences and learn how to handle them well. Facing those conflicts and not trying to evade from them, by facing those problems will bring resentments and solve the problems. If they are ignored or set aside, they will convert themselves into seeds of bitterness and resentment which can even destroy the much-treasured relationship. However, to resolve the conflict, they need to accept each other as they are. One should not ever try to attempt to create husband in wife image and wife into husband image. Rather, cultivate mutual respect and caring, show courtesy and politeness to one another, and willingness to compromise and change. In a love relationship there is forgiveness and reconciliation. Hurts and wounds can be healed with forgiveness and strengthen its relationship.[11]

Building healthy relationship within

Couples of interfaith marriages may likely experience compatibility difficulties. Their marriage may have disappointment and dissatisfaction due to unbearable issues. Such difficulties are often discovered as an underlying source of conflict. However, couples can explore how to deal with this kind of difficulties and can also resolve by acceptance and understanding so that they can have good relationship with one another. They need to understand and accept their own and their partner's need for personal and emotional support and to respond appropriately and helpfully. Some couples have difficulty accepting problems, issues, fearfulness, sadness, disappointment, frustration, or other kinds of hurting in themselves or in their partner. Such couple doesn't support themselves or respond nurturing to the partner. Therefore, couples can increase their awareness of each other feelings and needs by experiencing his or her spouse feelings and talk about what he or she wants and need from his or her spouse. Then, it will develop healthy relationship within them.[12]

Recommendations for the church leaders

There are some Church leaders who considered interfaith marriage as sin. It might be true, and it might not be true, but the fact is that interfaith marriage is not an unpardonable sin. Of course, it is an irregular and a discouraging behavior yet there should be a way of dealing with it in a fair manner. Instead of condemning it outright one needs to keep a forgiving mind. Jesus went to the extent of proclaiming forgiveness to the one who was caught in sexual sin. If Jesus can forgive the woman who was caught in adultery, will he not have an open mind to people involved in interfaith marriage? Therefore, even the Church should not have negative attitude towards those couples. They rather need to extent its care and concern beyond the boundary or beyond the four walls of the church with the conception of forgiveness.[13]

Extend responsibility in and outside of the church members

The task of the Christian church is to find positive ways of controlling and guiding forces of change so that the new values in community life make relationships redemptive as well as liberating.[14] One of the characteristics of the Christian Church is to demonstrate God's love through human relationships. In the Christian fellowship a believer may find tangible expression of the supernatural grace that endows his/her life. The body of Christ is a partnership where people share a common devotion to Christ and have opportunity to connect their inward lives with outward conduct through the transforming power of the spirit. The Church is a school where human learns to live a new life.[15]The church should see to the needs of the community in general and Christian members by helping financially, materially as well as spiritually. It should also be a place where they receive healing of mind, soul and body. Jesus visited and has a conversation outside the walls of the Jews. In Jesus' time, law does not permit Jews to talk and share thing with Samaritan, which they considered as unclean. However, Jesus went and asked for water from the Samaritan (John 4: 7ff). Therefore, the church leaders also need to extend its responsibility in and outside of church.

Home visitation in and outside the church members

This is a specific way of caring and a therapeutic tool, as part of an overall long-term relationship plan, which brings the couples inside the ministry of the God's kingdom. Home visiting is necessary and useful in many situations. It is difficult for the couples of interfaith marriages to move from home and seek help from the Church leaders because they feel embarrassed due to their exclusion from church. There is a need for the church leaders to observe the family setting and it is not possible to know unless they visit.[16]Bible proves that our God visits to his people in their circumstances, surrounding and situations (Gen.18:1-16). Even Jesus often visited people in their homes, to listen their problems and to build up the relationship (Mk.1:29-34; 5:35-43). Thus, pastoral visitation is an intangible way of relating the gospel to family life, irrespective of Church membership and religions. This visitation ties up with the person's need for help, protection, relationship and provide the sense of being care. It also fosters good rapport, a close affinity and made the person/family more comfortable to live and make it realize that there is somebody to care for their lives.[17] W. McFerrin Stowe testified that, "when we were in crushed due to child delivery, Pastor Jim Henley came to visit us in hospital. I shall never forget it and shall ever love him for his obvious caring when a young couple was devastated. His greatness to me is, his coming to us when we were so desolate and needed him so. The Pastor is the one who has the privilege of coming in the time of desolation."[18] Thus, church leaders or pastoral visitation is a way of comforting, concerning and also of caring others.

Extend love in and outside of the church members

Love is what people need more than anything else. Since God's love is for everyone irrespective of race, gender, religion and status, even the love of the Christians needs to be extended to everyone irrespective of own Church members and of diverse religions. Mother Teresa is called the saint of the gutters because she and her co-workers pick up the dying from the streets, tend them and help them realize that someone cares. She says that, more than food or medicine people need to come face to face with love. Everyone receives love from God freely. Therefore, everybody's love should be given freely to others as well. Everyone is born with the yearning to be loved and they need this love more than anything else. The couples of interfaith marriages too need love from others. They need to be cared by others because they are careless couples. As Jesus came loving people so also Christians should love other despite their fellow Christians and non-Christians.[19]

Maintain relationship in and outside of the church members

The Church should have interest in reaching beyond the walls of its own Church and nearby community. The Church must affirm the burden or call that God has given to everyone. This burden will always lead them to the lost with compassion to bring them in good relationship with the society and with the Lord. In writing to Colossians, Paul explained that he was not only a minister to the body of Christ, the church but also a minister to every creature which is under heaven (Col.1:23). John Wesley's famous declaration as cited by Vaidyan, "win the world for Christ at any cost" must be the Church's burning desire. In order to attract people for Christ, he has to behave properly toward outsiders (I Thess. 4:11,12). The church's lifestyle should declare a standard of integrity to the world. Church message to the world should be complete and its conduct in secular circumstances should be blameless and prudent, an example of honesty, diligent and respect. The Church must maintain a good reputation with those outside of the Church (I Tim. 3:7). This is the result of living an excellent testimony for those outside of the church. They must have a reputation in areas of business, community relations and civil law. They must be an example of Christian virtue in the world, at least to his close community in regard to integrity, honesty and purity. Churches are the light of the world, so should shine they should be not be bias with the active and non-active members of the church.[20]

Provide psychological aid in and outside of the church

Psychological aid is an evidence informed modular approach to help any person who are psychologically affected. Psychologically aid is designed to reduce the initial distress caused by traumatic events or by unfortunate incidents. It includes basic information gathering techniques from others to implement supportive activities in a flexible manner. It emphasizes developmentally, culturally, socially and spiritually appropriate interventions for survivors of various ages and backgrounds. It also includes handouts that provide important information for their better use in future to cope effectively with the psychological impact. The advantages of psychological aid are to establish a human connection in a non-intrusive, compassionate manner. It comforts them, make them calm and emotionally overwhelms them. It requires support adaptive coping efforts and strength and encourages them to take active role in their recovery. The counselor or the Church leaders who contact them should speak calmly, have patience in listening verbally and feeling as well, be responsive and sensitive, speak slowly and should not use acronyms and Jargon in their words. Remember that the goal of psychological aid is to reduce distress, assist with current needs and promote adaptive functioning.[21]

Organize marriage and family enrichment programmes

The Churches are advised to organize marriage and family enrichment programmes in and outside of the Church, addressing issues of conflict resolution, improving communication and intimacy and organising stress management and relaxation workshops to help the distress couples, to improve the couple communication and relationship with each other and with the family and the society. Such programmes have the possibility to reduce the friction between couples and of the in-laws, as they enriched the knowledge to overcome all the possible issues.[22]

Recommendations for the unmarried youth

As per the author's findings, there are more advantages to have same faith marriage than the interfaith marriage. It is because:

Same faith marriage has more advantage to understand each other

Everyone's life is moulded and governed by religion in one way or the other. The teaching of its religion is impacted in its heart. This becomes one of the bases to easily understand one's feeling and opinion from the same faith as they are brought up under the teaching of one faith. Thus, there is less possibility to take in negative sense which in return gives less space for creating conflict. Sometimes, as married couples, they should be able to read minds and sense unexpressed thoughts and feelings. The ability to do this is a strong indication of love and understanding.[23]

Same faith marriage has more advantage to forgive each other

Humans cannot exempt totally from the worldly problems. Even within the couples or within the family, there will be always a confusion period as they enter to new world and strive for the new better future. As they step into another unfamiliar spot, sometimes misunderstanding may occur, verbal war can be exchanged due to diverse interest and diverse concept. However, if the couples happen to be from the same faith, there are more chances to forgive one another as they develop such courage since the inception of their learning. In fact, for Christians forgiveness is one of the core themes to put on into one's life. Therefore, when there is forgiveness, naturally conflict ends.

Same faith marriage has more advantage in parenting

Mostly, the couples' way of molding their own child reflects from where and how they were molded up. More importantly, every religion has its own way of teaching children, way to raise the children and this bounded children in their lives. When two persons from different faith came together as couple, they find it difficult in adjusting the method and the way of raising children. There are contradictions among spouse as they are brought up with different method. And these contradictions among the spouse confuses the children and they begin the process of partiality or develop the sense of favouritism. Moreover, human's life is almost bounded by religious teaching because religious teaching covers the good and evil, the right and the wrong. The couple from same faith feels free to teach its religious teaching towards children which also leads children throughout their lives. Whereas, couples of interfaith marriages are hesitating to teach its own religious teaching which makes the children free child.

Same faith marriage has more advantage in planning together for future development

Life is not for a day, present alone cannot make one's life complete. It always goes along with past and future. Past struggle makes present comfortable, present proper planning will make future bright. Human without vision has no value of life. Same as, even couples have plan for future betterment and to do this it involves proper planning and wise decision making. Majority of the people's wisdom and conscience is developed from scripture. Planning is always directed by human conscience. In simple sense, human conscience is the starring of human's life. Thus, when the couples are from the same faith there is more advantage in planning together for future development because both the spouse's conscience was developed from the same root.

Common challenges for the couples of interfaith-marriage

Those who go for interfaith marriage will face different kinds of challenges and problems more than of those with same faith marriage. Some of the common challenges that the couples of interfaith marriage normally experience are learning to live with multiple beliefs, rituals, cultures and religious expectations in one home, difficulty in making decisions as parents about how to raise children as they come from different religious backgrounds, creating a "team marriage" where each partner maintains his or her integrity without impinging upon the integrity of the other, finding difficulty in negotiating how they will celebrate holidays and life cycle moments and difficulty in learning new communication skills to reflect both love and respect for their partner's religion and effectively communicate their individual religious needs at the same time.[24] Due to all these challenges, sometimes, couples of interfaith marriage ends up creating its own unique religious lifestyle.

Preparing to know the will of God

God creating Eve for Adam is not for sex alone, but it is for procreation, happiness and peace (Pr. 18:22; 19:14; 31:10-12). Christian should have the direct leading of God about marriage plans. A successful marriage must be based on genuine heart agreement of the couple who marry. A public witness wedding is a good start toward a happy marriage.[25] It is good to know the will of God for the right person. It is because people find meaning in the marriage. Whoever have married wrong person will never find real meaning in marriage. The meaning here is to the purpose of life, the happiness of living. Marriage is a lifelong companionship, physically, emotionally and spiritually and also God has a plan and purpose for each and every one to live a meaningful life. Therefore, to know the will of God, submit your feeling and interest before God, pray constantly to receive inspiration of the direction according to his will.

Approval of parents before the marriage

Happy is the young man and woman who finds ahead of time God's plan for the home and sets out to follow it. Bible standard for marriage as well as home needs are to be understood before the marriage. Marriage is not on the basis of contract as of business deal nor a brief experiment, rather it is of lifetime.[26] It is wise to take approval from the parents before stepping into marriage. Every parent has their own wish for the children, which is also adjustable. Sudden shock of parents by children's marriage may hurt them physically, emotionally and it may even effect in future relationship. Therefore, it is good not to rely always on personal interest and feelings and it is important to consider the interest of parents too.

Seek blessing

Seeking blessing from the parents, elders and the church leaders is one way to live a happy life and prosperous life. This blessing is mostly received by those who go along with their consent. The blessing of parents, elders and of the church ministers is always accompanied by God's blessing. God's blessing flows into the life of the husband and wife through the prayers of the parents and of the believers. Indeed, their blessing covers in all aspects of wisdom, good health, relationship and long life etc. Couples who receives blessing have the wisdom to face and handle different kinds of issues. And they have the courage to build broken relationships and they also have the knowledge to make wise plan for bright prospects.

Choosing right mate

In these days, careful choice of life partner and the commitment to live with one's chosen mate for better has been replaced with a self-centered attitude which sees marriage as a convenient living arrangement which always can be terminated if love grows cold. There are Biblical guidelines for choosing a right mate. It is clear from the scripture that believers are not to marry non-Christians. II Corinthians 6: 14 says, "Do not be mismatched with unbelievers. For what partnership is there between righteousness and lawlessness? Or what fellowship is there between light and darkness..." this is a clear warning that the Christians and the non-Christians cannot pull together as a marriage partner. Paul further states that the unmarried youths are free to marry whomever he/she wants but should be of the same believers. The second principles concern divine guidance. Abraham's servant experienced divine leading in selecting a wife for Isaac. Even today, we can expect that God will lead in selecting mate. Making wise choices certainly give a solid foundation on which to begin building of one's marriage. Marriage involves effort, risk and sometimes disappointment. These are not easy experiences, but it is more pleasant and motivating to work with a compatible teammate in life than with someone who apparently was a wrong choice.[27]

Towards the major predicaments, recommendations were made for three groups; couples of interfaith marriages, church leaders and for the unmarried youth. The possible ways to cope with the issues can be adopting the sense of couple as one body. If so, although the differences arises, they will have the capacity to understand as gifts and can adjust for better living. They need to have the courage facing all possible issues because only from that issues understanding, and healthy relationship exist. On the other side, the church leaders need to practice wholistic ministries, irrespective of one's faith. Their responsibility and concern have to reach out equally for everybody, both active and passive members. Lastly, recommendations were made for the unmarried youth to go for same faith marriage as there are more chances to understand each other's feeling leading to forgiveness and directing towards living harmoniously in terms of parenting as well. Therefore, before taking further steps, preparing to know the will of God and seeking blessing is a genuine step for lifetime marriage.

Endnotes

[1] Norbert, "Firewall in marriage," *Campus Link: Marriage matters,* Vol.14, No.3, May-June 2012, 16-17.

[2] Stephen Victor, "Intimacy in marriage," *Campus Link: Marriage matters,* Vol.14, No.3, May-June 2012, 21.

[3] Reuben, *There's an Easter egg on your Seder plate,* 58.

[4] John, *Spirituality of Marriage,* 145.

[5] Reuben, *There's an Easter Egg on your Seder Plate,* 38.

[6] Reuben, *There's an Easter Egg on your Seder Plate,* 172.

[7] S. Deveraj, *Parenting Skills in just 31 days* (Mumbai: St Pauls publications, 2013), 22. (Hereafter, Deveraj, *Parenting skills in just 31 days*).

[8] Melinda Haley, "Parenting Tips for Successful Discipline," http://www.twu.edu (accessed 16 November 2015).

[9] Deveraj, *Parenting skills in just 31 days,* 23.

[10] Samip Baruah, "A mother-in-law, daughter-in-law relationship," *Campus Link: Marriage matters,* Vol.14, No.3, May-June 2012, 32.

[11] Mary Thomas, *On the Threshold of Marriage* (New Delhi: ISPCK, 1989), 61.

[12] Barry K. Estadt, *Pastoral Counseling* (New Jersey: Prentice-Hall, Inc., Englewood Cliffs, 1983), 193-194.

[13] Sahanam, *Belonging but not Believing:* Interfaith marriage, 108.

[14] Mary Thomas, *Family Life, A Christian Perspectives* (Madras: The Christian Literature Society,1982),7.

[15] Samuel Southhard, "The Purpose of the Church and Its Counseling Ministry," in *An Introduction to Pastoral Counseling,* edited by Wayne E. Oates (Nashville: Broadman Press,1959), 28.

[16] UN refugee Agency, "Psychosocial counseling and social work with clients and their families in the Somali context," http://www.grtitalia.org (accessed on 11.11.2015).

[17] David K. Switzer, *the minister as crisis counselor* (Nashvilee: Abingdon Press, 1983), 103.

[18] W. Mcferrin Stowe, *If I were a Pastor* (Nashville: Abingdon press, 1983), 30. (Hereafter, Stowe, *If I were a Pastor*).

[19] Stowe, *If I were a Pastor*, 42.

[20] Vaidyan, *A Pastoral Theology and Manual* , 101.

[21] National Child Traumatic Stress Network, "Psychological First aid for community religious professionals," http://www.netsnet.org.pdf (accessed on 23rd October 2015).

[22] John, *Spirituality of Marriage*, 147.

[23] Yeo, *Partners in Life*, 23.

[24] Reuben, *There's an Easter egg on your Seder plate*, 95.

[25] E. Nrio Ezung, *Socio-cultural Theology of Marriage in Tribal context* (Nagaland: Kyong Baptist Ekhumkho Sanrhyutsu, 2009),93.

[26] Ezung, *Socio-cultural Theology of Marriage in Tribal context*, 95.

[27] Gary R. Collins, *Christian Counseling: A Comprehensive Guide* (Texas: Word Books Publisher, 1980). 148.

Conclusion

In a Pluralistic place where different people and different religious group from different places come for education, business and for job, there is a tendency to have interfaith marriages. This book digs out the issues that prevails among the couples of interfaith marriages, psychologically and socially in parenting. One of the main objectives of writing this book is to let the couples of interfaith marriages realize and acknowledge the problems, to tackle the problems wisely and to let the church leaders re-examine their ministry, especially towards the couples of interfaith marriages. The universal understanding of marriage is, "two persons seeking to form a more perfect life by giving themselves totally to each other." Thus, in marriage two persons look for better life for the better lifetime union. No doubt, this book is not to justify the true way of marriage rather it focusses on the problems faced by the couples of interfaith marriages and to give response from pastoral care and counseling with practical suggestions.

In these present days, couples of interfaith marriages increases because majority of the parents send their children to the mixed culture cities for education, where children lives in freedom without the guidance of parents and parents also do not have time to teach and guide them in God's way. As they are brought up in such mixed culture and environment, their attitude towards other religion become narrow, leading them to have love affairs with people of other faith. At present, youngsters do not care much about the issues of interfaith marriage and about one's faith. Rather more focus is given on one's profession because their interest lays on the better life and future prospect.

The couples of interfaith marriage experiences different kinds of problems which the couple of same faith marriage normally does not have. They experienced anxiety disorder like irrational fear, psychological traumas like a life-threatening situation, this also leads them to panic disorders and resulted to shortness of breath, dizziness and fear of dying. It develops guilt with major depression due to oppositions from the in-laws and misunderstanding among the couples. At last, these couples mostly end up in futureless and aimless life because they are empowered by the inferiority complex. As they come from different religious and cultural background, they have cross cultural adjustment issue. Thus, sometimes they are not willing to be with the society, at the same time, the society is also not willing to accept them totally as active citizens. This widens the relationship gap between these couples and the society and it isolates them. They have a hard time in adjusting day to day lifestyle, eating habits, interest, belief and celebration as they are brought up from different background and environment. Thus, misunderstanding and hatred are easily developed. Sometimes, human's lives are being lost due to this kind of marriage as the parents do not agree to this kind of marriage, and it has also a high tendency of divorce. Their issues will not end in their life alone but will extend till children's life, particularly in parenting. It is because every ethical teaching is mostly based on religious teaching and for many people, religious teaching is the foundation of one's life. These couples are confused over which religious teaching to teach and after all even the children are confused more. Therefore, sometimes these children end up without any religion which in returned effect their faith identity. These couples and children do not have close relationship with the religious leaders as they do not belong faithfully to any religion. Thus, in most of the areas these couples always become the victim.

At this juncture, effective response from pastoral care and counseling is highly required. The response is from the perspective of encouragement to live a better life, supportive for their good life experiences and advices should be given to take good care of themselves and precautions should be given before they face crucial experiences. Proper pastoral care should be given to those couples and families as the ministry of pastoral care is mutual healing and growth within and outside of its citizens. In other words, it is a wholistic ministry irrespective of diverse culture and faith. Christian counseling does not mean counseling only Christian fellow beings, rather it should extend its responsibility outside the walls of the Christians. Since, counseling is a process of healing (from both sides), it requires technique from different approaches as the issues differ from one another. Most importantly, extending counseling is not only to bring healing of the present issues but also to provide skills and techniques to handle the possible upcoming issues.

The suggestions were made for the couples, in order to prevent and handle such unfavorable incidents and to have the understanding that couples are one body. The differences in their lives come due to different creation but it compliments one another. Their differences is a gift from God and it is not a trouble or barrier in life because it makes them realize the uniqueness of themselves and makes them think deeper. Once they cultivate the differences as opportunity for them, there is possibility to live in harmony because they will never run away from the conflict rather, they will face it with multiple means to resolve. Thus, they will have the capability to build healthy relationship within the spouse and among the in-laws. On the one side, the church leaders should not have negative attitude towards those couples and families. Rather they should extend their love and concern. Their responsibility, their task, their love should reach even those couples and families to build better rapport and should provide all the possible help by organizing different kinds of programmes for their better future. At last, the youngsters should be aware of all these issues that happened in this kind of marriage. Therefore, same faith marriage has more advantage than the interfaith marriage because same faith marriage has the quality to understand each other, it has the sympathy to forgive each other and have the strength to plan together for future development. Hence, it is a wise decision for the youngsters to know the will of God before going for marriage by taking approval from the parents along with blessings and witness the right mate.

Appendix

DEMORGRAPHIC DATA

Age : (   )   Gender: Male/ Female

Religion : Past (   ) Present (   )

Age at Marriage: (   )   Profession: (   )

1. I feel that I am not a right person for my partner

Agree	Disagree	Don't know	Total
20	66	14	100

2. I do not feel comfortable with my spouse's parents

Agree	Disagree	Don't know	Total
32	68	0	100

3. Usually I have difficulty to sleep because of tensions in life.

Agree	Disagree	Don't know	Total
42	54	4	100

4. I feel over burdened in life

Agree	Disagree	Don't know	Total
40	26	4	100

5. I am always stressed about my spiritual life

Agree	Disagree	Don't know	Total
58	38	4	100

6. I am always worried about what is going to happen for my family in the future

Agree	Disagree	Don't know	Total
76	24	0	100

7. I always fear that our children also may end up in interfaith marriage later

Agree	Disagree	Don't know	Total
48	31	21	100

8. I am terribly upset with my family life that I think for divorce very often.

Agree	Disagree	Don't know	Total
18	70	12	100

9. I do feel that I miss my family members because of my interfaith marriage

Agree	Disagree	Don't know	Total
62	32	6	100

10. I yearn for somebody to visit and spend time with me.

Agree	Disagree	Don't know	Total
60	28	12	100

11. I do not have close friends after marriage.

Agree	Disagree	Don't know	Total
48	42	10	100

12. Society have not accepted us totally.

Agree	Disagree	Don't know	Total
45	41	14	100

13. My parents rejected us and are unwilling to share the property due to our interfaith marriage.

Agree	Disagree	Don't know	Total
34	56	10	100

14. There is no one whom I can talk and share about my day to day problems.

Agree	Disagree	Don't know	Total
50	48	2	100

15. I don't want to participate in any social gathering because they rejected me.

Agree	Disagree	Don't know	Total
28	62	10	100

16. I don't feel like going out.

Agree	Disagree	Don't know	Total
48	52	0	100

17. I have a low status because of my inter faith marriage.

Agree	Disagree	Don't know	Total
54	38	8	100

18. There is communication gap between society and us.

Agree	Disagree	Don't know	Total
12	74	14	100

19. My children do not listen to my advice.

Agree	Disagree	Don't know	Total
20	52	28	100

20. I am not able to raise my children well because of our difference in religious identity.

Agree	Disagree	Don't know	Total
38	54	8	100

21. We could not give good advices to our children due to diverse interest.

Agree	Disagree	Don't know	Total
34	40	26	100

22. Me and my partner disagree many times in punishing our children.

Agree	Disagree	Don't know	Total
44	50	6	100

23. Children are confused of their cultural identity.

Agree	Disagree	Don't know	Total
42	40	18	100

24. Children hardly share their prevalent issues.

Agree	Disagree	Don't know	Total
54	38	8	100

Bibliography

Books

Anthony, D. John. *Psychotherapies in Counseling: Includes Theories of Personality.* Tamil Nadu: Anugraha Publications, 2003.

Antony, John. *Family Counseling: the classic school.* Tamil Nadu: Anugraha Publications, 2005.

Ayeh, Aboli H. *Counseling the adolescents.* Mokokchung: Tribal Development and communication Centre, 2014.

Brewer, David Instone. *Divorce and remarriage in the Bible: The social and literary context.* Grand Rapids: William Eerdmans Publishing Company, 2002.

Chandran, J. Russell.*Christian Ethics.* New Delhi: ISPCK,2011.

Clebsch William A. and Jaekle, Charles R. *Pastoral Care in Historical perspective: An essay with exhibits with a new preface by the authors.* New York: Harper & Rows publishers, 1964.

Clinebell Howard J. and Clinebell, Charlotte H. *The intimate Marriage.* New York: Harper and Row Publishers, 1970.

Clinebell, Howard. *Basic types of Pastoral Care and Counseling.* Nashville: Abingdon Press, 1984.

Collins, Gary R. *Christian Counseling: A comprehensive guide.* Texas: Word Books Publisher, 1980.

Corey, Gerald. *Theory and Practice of Counseling and Psychotherapy.* Boston: Cengage Learning, 1976.

Crabb, Larry. *Effective Biblical Counseling.* Hyderabad: Authentic Books, 2011.

Das, Sanghita. *North Eastern Insurgency problems of assessment.* New Delhi: Anmol Publication, 2012.

Dennis Rainey, *Preparing for marriage.* California: Gospel Light publishing house, 1977.

Deveraj, S. *Parenting skills in just 31 days.* Mumbai: St Pauls publications, 2013.

Edison, Y.M. *Pastoral Counselling.* New Delhi: ISPCK, 2011.

Estadt, Barry K. *Pastoral Counseling.* New Jersey: Prentice-Hall, Inc., Englewood Cliffs, 1983.

Ezung, E. Nrio. *Socio-cultural theology of Marriage in Tribal context.* Nagaland: Kyong Baptist Ekhumkho Sanrhyutsu, 2009.

Floyd, Scott. *Crisis Counseling: A guide for Pastors and Professionals.* Grand Rapids, Kregel Publications, 2008.

Guerrero, Anna Leon . *Social problems: community, policy and social action.* New Delhi: SAGE Publications, 2009.

James, Emmanuel E. *"Ethics: A Biblical perspective."* Bangalore: Theological Book Trust, 2001.

Jamir, Imtijungla. *Restore our family.* Nagaland: Disciples Bible College, 2006.

John, Santhos. *Spirituality of marriage.* Delhi: ISPCK, 2011.

K.Kay, William. Weaver, Paul C. *Pastoral Care and Counseling.*Secunderabad: OM Authentic books, 2007.

Kath, Phananmo. *Human Sexuality: Endangered morality in Cybersonic era.* Mokokchung: TDCC, 2013.

Kath, Phanenmo. *"Homosexuality: A challenge to Christian Homes,"* in *Introducing Challenges to modern Concern.* Edited by Narola Imchen. Jorhat: Tribal Women Study Centre, 2010.

Kithan, Zubeno.*Pastoral care and counseling.* West Bengal: SCEPTRE, 2013.

Lahaye, Tim. *How to win over Depression.* Secunderabad; Authentic Books, 2008.

Luck, William F. *Divorce and Remarriage: Recovering the Biblical view.* San Francisco: Harper and Row Publisher, 1987.

Lutzer, Erwin W. *The Truth about Same Sex Marriage.* Andhra Pradesh: OM books, 2012.

Macarthur, John. *The divorce dilemma: God's last word on lasting commitment.* Maharashtra: Grace to India, 2009.

Mannarkulam, Anthony. *Hand Book of Counseling and Psychotherapies.* Kottayam: Sanjivani Rehabilitation Center, 1997.

Morgan, Cliffort T. *Introduction to Psychology.* New Delhi: McGraw Hill Education Pvt. Ltd., 2014.

Murry, Ezamo. *An introduction to Pastoral Care and Counseling.* New Delhi: ISPCK, 2009.

Murry, Ezamo. *An Introduction to Pastoral care and Counseling.* New Delhi: ISPCK, 2009.

Neukrug, Edward. *Counseling Theory and Practice.* New Delhi: Cengage Learning, 2012.

Rainey, Dennis. *Preparing for marriage.* California: Gospel Light publishing house, 1977.

Raju, I.J. Mohan. *Christian Social Ethics: Issues, Dilemmas, Applications and Responses.* Mokokchung: CCPRA, 2015.

Rao, C.N. Shankar. *Sociology : Principles of Sociology with an Introduction to social thought.* New Delhi: S.Chand and Company Pvt. Ltd, 2011.

Rao, S. Narayana. *Counseling Psychology.* New Delhi: Tata McGraw Hill Publishing Company Limited,1984.

Reuben, Steven Carr. *There's an Easter egg on your Seder plate.* West port, Praeger publisher, 2008.

Sahanam, L.E. *Belonging but not Believing: Interfaith marriage.* New Delhi: ISPCK, 2009.

Steward, Charles William. *The Minister as Marriage Counselor: A role-relationship theory of marital Counseling and Pastoral Care.* Nashville: Abingdon press, 1983.

Stewart, Charles William. *The Minister as marriage counselor.* Nashville: Abingdon Press, 1970.

Stowe, W. Mcferrin. *If I were a Pastor.* Nashville: Abingdon press, 1983.

Switzer, David K. *The minister as crisis counselor.* Nashvilee: Abingdon Press, 1983.

Thomas, Juliet. *Raising Children God's way.* Secunderabad: OM Books, 2002.

Thomas, Mary. *Family Life, A Christian Perspectives.* Madras: The Christian Literature Society, 1982.

_____.*On the threshold of marriage.* New Delhi: ISPCK, 1989.

Thumra, Jonathan H. *Social and Religious Issues: An Analytical Study.* Ukhrul, Manipur: Tangkhul Theological Association, 2008.

Vaidyan, T.K. Koshy. *A pastoral theology and manual.* Hyderabad: Authentic books, 2013.

Worthington, Everett. *Christian Marital Counseling.* Secunderabad: OM books, 2002.

Yeo, Anthony. *Partners in life.* Goa: APECA Publications, 1993.

DICTIONARIES AND ENCYCLOPEDIA

Barker, Kenneth L. & John Kohlenberger, *Zondervan NIV Bible Commentary.* Grand Rapids, Michigan, Zondervan Publishing House, 1990.

Bandstra B.L. and Verhey, A.D. "Sex." *The International Standart Bible Encyclopedia,* ed. Geoffray W. Briley, Volume Four Q-Z. Grand Rapids: William B. Eerdmans Publishing Company, 1986.

Bower R.K. and Knapp, G.K. "Marriage." *The International Standart Bible Encyclopedia.*Ed. Geoffray W. Briley, Volume Three K-P. Grand Rapids: William B. Eerdmans Publishing Company, 1986.

Graham, L.K. "Healing." *Dictionary of Pastoral care and counseling.* Edited by Rodney J. Hunter. Bangalore: Theological Publications of India, 2007.

Hamilton, Victor P. "Marriage." *The Anchor Bible Dictionary.* Volume 4. Edited by David Noel Freedman, Gary A. Herion. New York: Doubleday publishing group, 1992.

Landrud, J.C. "Transactionl analysis." *Dictionary of Pastoral care and counseling.* Edited by Rodney J. Hunter.Bangalore: Theological Publications of India, 2007.

Murry, Ezamo."The role of Tribal Pastors towards Persons with disability."*Journal of Tribal Studies,* vol. xiv, No. 2 (2009).

Osmer, R.R. "Education, Nurture and Care." *Dictionary of Pastoral Care and Counseling.* Edited by Rodney J. Hunter. Bangalore: Theological Publications of India, 2007.

Perkin, Hazel W. "Marriage." *New International Bible Dictionary.* Edited by J. D. Douglas, Merrill C. Tenney. Grand Rapids,: Zondervan Publishing House, 1997.

Smith, William. "Marriage" *Smith's Bible Dictionary.* Edited by Francis and Mary Peloubet.Chattanooge: AMG Publishers, 2008.

Southhard, Samuel. "The Purpose of the Church and Its Counseling Ministry."*An Introduction to Pastoral Counseling.* Edited by Wayne E. Oates.Nashville: Broadman Press,1959.

Sullender, R.S. "Supportive counseling." *Dictionary of Pastoral Care and Counseling.* Edited by Rodney J. Hunter. Bangalore: Theological Publications of India, 2007.

Wright, J.S. "Marriage."*New Bible Dictionary.* Edited by J.D. Douglas, N. Hillyer. Illinois: Intervarsity press, 2003.

Wright, L. "Anxiety disorders." *Dictionary of Pastoral care and counseling.* Edited by Rodney J. Hunter.Bangalore: Theological Publication of India, 2007.

Journals and Periodicals

"Only Jesus is her boss," *The Gospel truth*, Hyderabad, India, (03rd July 2015).

"Pacquiao negotiating new deals after NIKE axe," *The Morung Express*, Nagaland, (24th February 2016).

"Transgender struggle in Nagaland," *The Morung Express*, Nagaland, (17th August 2015).

Baruah, Samip. "A mother-in-law, daughter-in-law relationship." *Campus Link: Marriage matters*, Vol.14, No.3, May-June 2012.

Beck, Julie. "How friendship fight depression." *The Morung Express*, Nagaland, August 21, 2015.

Kevichusa, Kethoser. "Forgiveness in the absence of justice and reconciliation: An ethical exploration with special reference to the issue of Naga Political murders." *Violence and Peace: Creating a culture of Peace in the contemporary context of violence.* Edited by Frampton F. Fox. Bangalore: Asian Trading Corporation, 2010.

Murry, Ezamo."The role of Pastors in caring for persons with disability."*Embracing the inclusive community: A disability perspective.* Edited by Wati Longchar and R. Christopher Rajkumar. Bangalore: SATHRI, 2010.

Norbert. "Firewall in marriage." *Campus Link: Marriage matters*, Vol.14, No.3, May-June 2012.

Southhard, Samuel. "The Purpose of the Church and Its Counseling Ministry." *An Introduction to Pastoral Counseling.* Edited by Wayne E. Oates. Nashville: Broadman Press, 1959.

Thomas, M.D. "Towards an identity beyond all identities." *Mission Today: Preaching and Teaching*, Vol. XVI. No.2 (April- June, 2014).

Victor, Stephen. "Intimacy in marriage." *Campus Link: Marriage matters*, Vol.14, No.3, May-June 2012.

Unpublished Thesis and Books

Enokali. "A study on the Psychological problems faced by childless couples among Sumi community: Implication for Pastoral Care and Counseling." M.Th. Thesis, Clark Theological College, Aolijen, Mokokchung, 2015.

National Commission for Women. "Issues relating to NRI marriages." VigyanBhawan, New Delhi: National Commission For Women , 2011.

Khuiso, Shimprui. "The elopement and its impact on the Tangkhul Naga society: A Christian Education perspective." M.Th. Thesis Eastern Theological College, Jorhat, 2015.

Sumi, Rebecca. "A study on the Psychological problems of widows in Sumi community: Implication for Pastoral Care and Counseling." M.Th. Thesis, Clark Theological College, Aolijen, Mokokchung, 2015.

Questionnaires

Aaron, RN. Pastor Mayophung Baptist Church, response to questionnaire, Ukhrul, 9th January 2016.

Jajo, Rinmayo. Pastor Riha Baptist Church, response to questionnaire, Ukhrul, 14th January 2016.

Jajo, Wilson. Pastor Wunghon Baptist Church, response to questionnaire, Ukhrul, 14th January 2016.

Raihing, Peimi. Women leader, Wunghon Baptist Church, response to questionnaire, Ukhrul, 14th January 2016.

Raihing, Wungmi. Associate Pastor, Wunghon Baptist Church, response to questionnaire, Ukhrul, 12th January 2016.

Shaizak, Ishmael. Pastor Wunghon Baptist Church, response to questionnaire, Ukhrul, 14th January 2016.

Zimik, Realson. Pastor Ramrei Aze Baptist Church, response to questionnaire, Ukhrul, 10th January 2016.

Zimik, Samuel. Pastor Ngarumphung Baptist Church, response to questionnaire, Ukhrul, 13th January 2016

Webliography

http://www.en.wikipedia.org (accessed on 23rd August 2015).

"Eloping packages" http://www.idoeventswhitsundays.com.au (accessed on 20th October 2015).

Reinheimer, Justin. "Same-Sex Marriage through the Equal Protection Clause: A Gender-Conscious Analysis", http://scholarship.law.berkeley.edu/bglj(accessed on 20th July 2015).

http://www.definitionuslegals.com (accessed on 20th July 2015).

http://www.en.wikipedia.org (accessed on 23rd August 2015).

George Davis, "A Biblical Response to Same-Sex Marriage", http://www.hersheyfree.com (accessed on 23rd August 2015).

Sprigg, Peter. "The top ten Harms of Same-sex marriage," http://www.download.frc.org.(accessed on 16th February 2016).

Keller, Tim. "The Bible and same sex relationships: A review article", http://www.redeemer.com (accessed on 23rd August 2015).

http://www.en.wikipedia.org (accessed on 23rd August 2015).

http://www.Timesofindia.indiatimes.com (accessed on 10 August 2015)

Arida, Robert M. "Response to myself" http://www.holytrinityorthodox.org (accessed on 23rd August 2015).

Davis, George. "A Biblical Response to Same-Sex Marriage", http://www.hersheyfree.com (accessed on 23rd August 2015).

Edmiston, John. "A Biblical Response to Same-sex marriage", http://www.globalchristian.org (accessed on 23rd August 2015).

"Common issues in mixed marriage." http://www.internations.orgn. (accessed on20/10/2014).

"Cross-Cultural navigation." http://www.googles.com (accessed on 22/10/2014).

"History of Jewish interfaith marriage." www.Interfaithfamily.com (accessed on 22.06.1015).

"Imphal East District: 2011 census Data." http://www.census2011.co.in (accessed on20/10/2014).

Abrahams, Naasiha. "Managing socio-religious expectations in an intimate space: Examining Muslim interfaith marriage amongst working class communities in Cape Town. Master of Social Science in Religious Studies Thesis, Faculty of the Humanities University of Cape Town, 2012.http//www.open.uct.ac.za (accessed on 22/06/ 2015).

Arnold, Johann Christoph. "Sex, God and Marriage." http//:www.ntslibrary.com (accessed on 10/07/2015).

Bishop conference of Indian and Wales. http://www.googles.com (accessed on 22/06/ 2015).

Centre for parenting and Research. "Effective parenting capacity assessment: key issues." http://www.community.nsw.gov.au (accessed on 11 September 2015).

Chapman, Kyle. "Interfaith Marriage Counseling: Perspectives and Practices among Christian Ministers." M.A. Thesis, Graduate Faculty of Texas Tech University, 2011. http://www.repositories.tdl.org (accessed on 16.10.2014).

Gasper, Sofia."Mixed marriages between European free movers." http//www.cles.iscte.pt. (accessed on 24/06/2015)

Haley, Melinda. "Parenting Tips for Successful Discipline." http://www.twu.edu (accessed 16 November 2015).

Immigration and Refugee Board of Canada. "India: Situation of inter-religious couples from both urban and rural locations, including societal attitudes, treatment by government authorities and the treatment of their children (2005-April 2012)." 11 May 2012. http://www.refworld.org (accessed 13 November 2014).

Kabamba,Tshibangulaiddyslas."The psycho-social challenges facing HIV/AIDS lay counsellors at a community-based voluntary counselling and testing site in Tshwane." M.A. Thesis, University of South Africa, 2009.http://www.uir.unisa.ac.za (accessed on 11.9.2015).

Migration and Refugees Review Tribunal Country Advice, "Mixed Marriage in India."http://www.refworld.org (accessed on 22/10/ 2014).

Migration Review Tribunal, "Mixed marriages in India."http://www.refworld.org (accessed 06 July 2015).

National Child Traumatic Stress Network. "Psychological First aid for community religious professionals." http://www.netsnet.org.pdf (accessed on 23rd October 2015).

Problems-mixed-marriages:http://www.ehow.com/about_5369857_html (accessed on 20/10/2014).

Romain, Jonathan. "The Effects of Mixed-Faith Marriages on Family Life and Identity." http//www.anthro.ox.aca (accessed on 24/06/15).

Schwartz, Allan. "The emotional challenges of interfaith marriage." http://www.googles.com (accessed on 22/10/ 2014).

Shaffer, Tammy J. "Interfaith Marriage and Counseling Implications." http:www.citeseerx.ist.psu.edu (accessed on 22/10/ 2014).

Stewart, Monte Neil. "Marriage Facts." http://www.law.harvard.edu (accessed 06 July 2015).

Terre, Elisha Hope. "Interfaith marriage and its effects on the family: A Jewish perspective." Master of Science Thesis, The Graduate Faculty University of Wisconsin-Platteville, 2012).http://www.googles.com (accessed on 22/10/ 2014).

Uddin, Mohammad Moin. "Inter-religious Marriage in Bangladesh: An Analysis of the Existing Legal Framework."The Chittagong University Journal of Law, Vol. XIII, 2008, p.117- 139. http://www.googles.com (accessed on 22/06/ 2015).

UN refugee Agency. "Psychosocial counseling and social work with clients and their families in the Somali context." http://www.grtitalia.org (accessed on 11.11.2015).

World Alliance of reformed Churches. "Theology of marriage and the problems of mixed marriages. "http://www.ecumenism.net (accessed 06 July 2015).